A NECESSARY END

A Novel of World War II

by Nathaniel Benchley

Harper & Row, Publishers
New York, Hagerstown, San Francisco, London

For N. R.

different war, same problems

Of all the wonders that I yet have heard,
It seems to me most strange that men should fear,
Seeing that death, a necessary end,
Will come when it will come.

—WILLIAM SHAKESPEARE,

—*Julius Caesar* [*II. 2. 34–37*]

CONTENTS

Note:

Television war coverage, although it brings one or two of the harsher realities of battle into the living room, is nevertheless incomplete in the overall picture, because the omniscience of the telecaster prevents his showing the confusions that occur throughout the lower strata. This is the story of one extremely small unit in a war that is hearsay to a whole generation, and a war that has been second-guessed so much there is a tendency to forget what it was really like. The men at the lower levels have no sense of global strategy; they have, very simply, the fervent hope they will survive the twin enemies of man: hostile action, and boredom.

—N.B.

1 · THE OUTFITTING

Monday, September 20, 1943—This seems like as good a time as any to start this diary. The folks sent it to me for my seventeenth birthday, which was two weeks ago, but the mails being what they are it didn't arrive until last Friday, and the weekend is no time to start a diary. Not that I *did* anything over the weekend (who could, in Key West?) but it seems sort of sloppy to start at the tag end of the week.

So here I am, finishing up at the Fleet Sound School. When I made Seaman First I told them I wanted to be a Signalman striker—that is, study for a Signalman's rating —because I'd heard that duty in the fresh air is less likely to make you seasick than if you're cooped up somewhere below decks. (I don't know if I'm going to be seasick or not, but the way I look at it there's no point asking for a thing like that if you don't have to. I mean, you've got enough to worry about in a war without worrying about where you throw your lunch.)

So they said sure, Bub, anything to make you happy,

and with that they ship me off to the Sound School, which is about the last thing in the world I want to do. A sonarman sits in a little nook off the bridge and operates the sound stack, a gizmo that sends out a "ping" through the water, and if there's a submarine or other solid object nearby an echoing "ping" bounces back. So the sonarman gives a "ping" every five degrees from beam to beam across the bow, and listens for an echo. *Ping*—train—listen—*ping*—train—listen—*ping*—train—listen—*ecccch*. In the meantime, he's like as not puking in his socks. I think when I get to my ship I won't tell them about being in Sound School. I'll just say I'm very big in signalling, and see what happens.

Tuesday, September 21, 1943—We were exercising with a tame sub today—an old O boat, from World War I—and almost ran it down. The dumb cluck surfaced dead ahead of us, and when he saw us he like to wet his pants. He went under again so fast his screws were spinning clear of the water. I'll bet that C.O. has a lot to explain tonight. It's fun to think of officers with their asses in a jam.

Nothing much else to report. They say we should be getting our orders pretty soon. With my luck, I'll probably be sent to a garbage barge in Kiska.

Wednesday, September 22, 1943—Got a letter from the folks today, asking if I'd received the diary. It was Dad who wrote the letter (what with the war and the lack of tourists, he has a lot of time to mope around the house), but I know it was Mom put him up to it. She can't stand it if she doesn't get a letter from me every two days, and what with one thing and another I just haven't had time to write. I haven't even written Alice, which will give an idea of how busy I've been.

Speaking of letters, I got a good one from Miss Gresham

the other day. She said she was sorry I'd quit school when I did, even though it was for patriotic purposes, because the way I'd been going in English she thought I might have wound up with an A for the year. That would have been something, to get my first A in the middle of a flock of Cs and Ds, not to mention an E or so. But I'm glad she thinks I joined up for patriotic reasons—if I was bone-deep honest I'd have to admit I joined up because things on Nantucket were deader than a squashed cat, and sooner or later the Draft would have got me anyway. But if she wants to think I'm all that patriotic that's finest kind—maybe she'll slip me that A when I get back. I hear that veterans get all sorts of breaks, so you never can tell.

Thursday, September 23, 1943—Spent practically the whole day on the Attack Teacher, which is a mockup of a ship's wheel house, complete with sound stack, wheel, chemical recorder, and all. The whole business is electronically controlled, with your "ship" and a "sub" shown on a screen in another room, and an instructor makes the "sub" move while you try to catch it. The chemical recorder tells you when to fire—or simulate firing—your charges, and then when the attack is over you go in the next room and look at the traces on the screen, and see how wrong you were. It's a fascinating gimmick the first hundred times you do it, but after the three millionth time you feel like you're doing the whole business under water (knock wood). It is just *some dull*, and that's all that can be said for it.

Got a letter from Alice today, telling how the football team got whipped by Provincetown, 32–0. Then after the game she went out with Slappy Souza and he borrowed his father's car and got it stuck in Nickerson's sand pits. She told me all about rationing and how hard it was to get decent food, and said she envied me the good food she

3

hears they give us in the Navy. At least she wrote, so I guess I can't complain. If nothing else, it was a letter.

Friday, September 24, 1943—It's amazing the new language you have to learn when you join the Navy. They have their own words for just about anything, and if you use a civilian word you either get chewed out by an officer or laughed at by the other guys. For instance, left and right are port and starboard—which I guess everyone knows—but then a drinking fountain is a scuttlebutt (and scuttlebutt also goes for gossip and rumors, which often start there), the can is the head, the ceiling is the overhead, ropes are lines, a staircase is a ladder, downstairs is below, upstairs is topside, front and back are forward and aft, crossways is thwartship, a gangplank is a brow (sometimes), a camel is a float between the ship and the dock, the bullnose is the loop up in the bow a towing hawser goes through, that stick across the mast is a yardarm, a monkey fist is the knot at the end of a heaving line, the floor is the deck, a map is a chart, a post is a stanchion, the rail is the lifeline, the word for stop is either avast or belay (you say, "Avast heaving," or "Belay that," in that case belay meaning "Forget it"), to stop a drill or exercise is to secure from it, to get rid of something is to survey it or—if throwing it over the side —to give it the deep six, and then there are all sorts of technical terms that lookouts use, giving relative bearings and angle of elevation. A lookout who just says, "Out there," and points, is going to find himself in deep trouble. I think I'll write a letter home, using nothing but Navy language, and see what happens.

Saturday, September 25, 1943—The last day of this class at Sound School. We had a Captain's inspection in the morning, with everybody in dress whites, and a couple of the student officers, who knew German, decided it would be a good joke to make a run in that language on the Attack Teacher, I was on the sound stack, and I heard the officer who had the conn say, *"Links zwanzig degrees Rutter!"* which the other officer, on the wheel, repeated after him, and then *"Feuer eins, feuer zwei,"* and so on. They did it just as the inspection party came through our section, and I thought the Captain was going to swallow a grapefruit. His eyes bugged out and he began to choke, but then the officer with the conn made a nearly perfect attack, so there wasn't much the Captain could do about it.

We secured at noon, and three of us went to the bar at the La Concha. But it was full of officers (one of whom had a kitten under his cap), so we went to some dump off Duval Street and drank beer until they called the Shore Patrol. We got out just before the Gestapo arrived, and took our business elsewhere. I'm not quite sure where, but there were long bead curtains, and red shades over the lights.

Sunday, September 26, 1943—Finally got my letters written. The idea of writing in Navy language didn't seem quite so funny today, so I wrote regular letters to the folks and to Alice, and then for good measure I wrote one to Miss Gresham and one to the girl I met in the Spa with Harry Coffin. Her name was Diane something-or-other, so all I could do was address it to her care of Harry. This was probably a stupid move, but the way I look at it I haven't lost anything. And if she should ever answer, so much the better. A letter is a letter, no matter who it comes from. (There's a sort of poem there, but I don't feel like writing poetry right now. Four letters and a diary is enough for one day.)

Monday, September 27, 1943—My orders arrived to-day, and I'm on a PC! This is a 173-foot subchaser, which generally works with slow coastal convoys, and it has the advantage of being big enough to handle the weather but not so big as to make a good target. I could have got an SC, which is a 110-foot wooden subchaser and all hell to live in, or I could have got a DE, which is almost like a destroyer and a tempting target for torpedoes (that's what Miss Gresham would call alliteration). A PC is just about the perfect size, and what's more on the coastal convoys you're in port about every two weeks. All in all, the whole thing is finest kind.

Thursday, September 30, 1943—Arrived at the Brooklyn Receiving Station today, after a trip by train, bus, truck, and who knows what. The ship is being built over at the Consolidated Shipyard, in the Bronx, and we have to wait here until it's ready for us. The way things go this could be a couple of months, and if they don't give us something to do we'll likely go crazy. All we get are calisthenics and then work details around the barracks, and a day of that kind of duty is as inspiring as a year on the Attack Teacher. Or Alcatraz.

The enlisted complement of a PC is sixty-one men, and right now there are about a dozen of us for the 1208 in the barracks. Some of the machinist's mates are off at the Diesel school in Ohio, and some of the gunnery guys are at the gun school in Newport, so those of us here are the unrated ones they can't think of anything to do with. None of us has ever been to sea, so we're all so to speak in the same boat (ha! ha!).

Monday, October 4, 1943—Suddenly, there seem to be a lot of 1208 men here. The gunners and the snipes (machinists) came back from their schools, other men came from other ships and stations, and now we're almost up to complement. The biggest surprise for me was to see, among

6

the snipes, none other than Pin-Head Gillis, whom I'd last seen a year ago on the Island. I'd always thought he was something of a drip—his one big achievement was to make the 7½ miles from 'Sconset into Town in four minutes flat, in a souped-up '38 Ford convertible—but now seeing some-one from home gave me a good feeling, and we greeted each other loudly, with a lot of "how ya doin's," and "well, for chrissakes," and things like that. He's a Motor Mach Third, and when I told him I was going to strike for Signalman he kind of sniffed and shrugged, said something about deck monkeys, then changed the subject. It was the Pin-Head I remembered—feeling a little above everyone else, although for no reason you could see with the naked eye.

The senior enlisted man in our group is a Chief Motor Mach named Rinaldi, a pot-bellied old timer with gold hash marks up to his elbow. He doesn't act so tough, but one look at all the gold and ribbons makes you jump to do whatever he says. (The gold hash marks, by the way, mean he's never been caught doing anything out of line. If he'd had one bad mark on his record, the hash marks would be red. This, when you consider he's been in for over twenty-five years, is some big achievement.)

Tuesday, October 5, 1943—This morning the Chief called us together and told us to make ourselves present-able, because the exec was coming over to see us. About a half hour later the exec showed up, and introduced himself as Mr. Ferguson. He's a full Lieutenant, tall and not very military looking, but he's got three area ribbons (pre-Pearl Harbor, American Theatre, and European Theatre) so I guess he's been around. He had a lot of papers with him and he passed them out saying they were questionnaires he'd like us to fill out, to help him make our assignments on

7

board ship. They were the usual sort of thing, asking your experience, your rate or what you were striking for, and all that, but there was also a question asking your hobbies, and I couldn't figure out the reason. I asked him, and he said, "It just gives me a hint. If you like to hunt, for instance, then you might go on a gun crew. If your hobby is electricity, you might be a telephone talker at General Quarters; if you're a carpentry nut, you'd be put on a damage-control party. That sort of thing."

"Damn," said Pin-Head. "I already put down 'girls.'"

We all laughed, and the exec smiled. "I'm afraid we can't help you there," he said.

I figured this was the time to strengthen my bid for Signalman, so under hobbies I put down "signalling," then handed in the form. I went back to my place, and the exec scanned my answers.

"Uh—Bowers," he said, after a moment.

"Yes, sir?" I replied.

"This hobby of yours. Just what do you do?"

"I—ah—signal, sir. You know—dit-dah . . ." I made fluttering movements with my hands.

"You mean radio?"

"No, sir!" Radio was even worse than sonar, as far as seasickness was concerned. "Just—well, light. And flags."

"With someone else?"

"Not necessarily. I just like to—signal."

He gave me a long look, and I could feel myself turning red. Then someone else handed in his paper, and the exec forgot about me. I think there's a lesson here somewhere, and it's called don't get too smart too fast.

Thursday, October 7, 1943—Today five of us went to the Fire Fighting School, and it's a day I won't forget in a hurry. The captain wants every man on board to take the

8

two-day course, because he feels everyone should know how to put out a fire. I suppose he's right, but I don't see a PC as being a likely ship to be shot at with incendiary shells. At any rate, we went over to the Navy Yard, where they have a steel-and-brick building, the inside of which is compartmented off like a ship, with steel ladders, catwalks, and the rest, and the whole cellar is loaded with Diesel oil. Well, sir, what do they do but prime the oil with gasoline, set it on fire, and then when the fire is really roaring they send us into it, wearing only boots, slickers, and rain hats, and carrying only a fire hose with a fog nozzle, which makes a fine mist-like spray that believe it or not puts out the fire. First you hose down the doorway until it's just smoke and steam, then you move into this furnace, spraying all around you, until finally the thing is out. There's a professional fireman with you to see you don't do anything stupid (like letting the fire re-start behind you), but that doesn't make it any less scary. I swear to God I've never been so terrified as I was the first time we went in. I was last man on the hose, but next time the man on the nozzle moved back and each man moved up one, so pretty soon I was on the nozzle, and peeing green. There was an Ensign from the 1208 with us, a Mr. Murray, and I'm glad to say he seemed as scared as the rest of us. He looks about twelve years old.

Friday, October 8, 1943—Today was almost a disaster. A southern kid named Gibbon slipped off the catwalk and fell into the smoking oil, but before he could so much as get singed Mr. Murray reached down, grabbed him by the collar of his slicker, and yanked him back up onto the catwalk. Gibbon's eyes were as big as baseballs but he didn't say anything; he just wrapped his arms around the hose, and on we went into the fire. Mr. Murray is the Communications Officer, which means he'll be head of my division, and that's a comforting thing to know. We finished the day on the roof of the building, while they set a fire beneath us, and we had to try to put it out by squirting water down the mockup ventilators, hatches, and so on. I can tell one thing right now, and that is there can be no fire on any PC as big as the fires I've been through in the last two days. They say all fires are the same size when they start, but I've been through the granddaddies of them all. Maybe that's the point of the course.

On the way back through the Navy Yard we saw the cruiser *Marblehead*, an old four-piper that got beaten up by the Japs out around Borneo last year. She's pretty well repaired now, but they say the damage was so bad she had to make straight for home, without even taking time to bury the dead. They just welded the damaged compartments and turrets shut, so no air could get through, and left the guys in there until they got back. What it was like when they opened up, I'd rather not think.

Thank God we're not going to the Pacific.

Monday, October 11, 1943—I got a break today. Word came from the ship they wanted a couple of men to come help correct the charts, so Linkovitch, who's a Quartermaster Third, and I got a ride on a Navy truck that was going to Consolidated Shipyard. Linkovitch had been on the *Oklahoma* at Pearl Harbor, and when she overturned he and some other guys were trapped in the lazarette for twenty-four hours. I asked him what it was like, and he shrugged. "You get used to it," he said. "We had battle lanterns, so mostly we played acey-deucey." Every now and then they'd bang on the hull, to make sure people knew they were there, and finally some guys with cutting torches made a hole big enough for them to climb out. I asked him what he, a battleship man, was doing on a PC, and he grinned. "Survivors get their choice of new construction," he said. "I asked for something small, that nobody'd bother to shoot at." That made me feel good. From the little I've seen and heard, being shot at can lead to all sorts of trouble.

Consolidated is in the Bronx, on the banks of the Harlem River, and the first thing we saw was a big clutter of low buildings, and in the ways and at the docks were a number of PCs in various stages of construction. You could see the blue lights of the welders' torches, and the air banged with the sound of riveters' hammers, and the whole place seemed about as disorganized as a Legion clambake. The ship ahead of ours, the 1207, looked almost finished and glistened with new paint, but although the 1208's hull was painted the superstructure looked like a shanty in a junk yard, and it was hard to believe she'd ever go to sea. We asked around, and were told to go in the main building, where our ship had been assigned a small office. We went (continued tomorrow)

Tuesday, October 12, 1943—where we were told, and found Mr. Ferguson and the captain, a short, dark-haired man with heavy eyebrows. He's also a full Lieutenant but much senior to the exec; Mr. Ferguson's new stripe is all bright and shiny, but the captain's stripes are dull and tarnished looking. He's quiet, but seems to know what he's doing (knock wood).

Our job is to take a stack of copies of *Notice to Mariners*, a monthly bulletin that shows all the changes that have been made in channels, buoys, lights, and whatnot—as well as new wrecks—and make these changes on our charts so as to bring them up to date. It's a long, dull job, but at least it gets us away from the Receiving Station during the daytime, and gives us a change of scenery. I never realized the amount of paper work that goes into a ship—the inventories, the lists of spare parts, the personnel forms, the reports, the orders—it's more like being in an accounting house than a ship. The office smells of varnish and steam heat, which gives you a headache after a while.

On a hill, across the river from the yard, there's a big brick building that looks something like a school. It's surrounded by trees which are now beginning to change their colors, and I must say I never thought I'd be so happy to see the reds and oranges and yellows of autumn. After a few weeks in Florida, where all you see are dusty, brittle palm trees, the sight of an honest-to-God tree is exciting. It made me think of the autumn moors at home, when the whole Island seems to turn red and yellow, and I felt my first real twinge of homesickness. I thought how the bass go crazy at the time of the Hunter's Moon, when the sun sets just as the full moon is rising, and I thought of the pheasant season, and the taste of raw scallops you've just picked out of Polpis Harbor, and the ring of shiny little blue eyes around a scallop's mantle, and the smell of wood fires, and pretty soon I was in a real, low-down, blue funk. The water of the Harlem River has absolutely nothing in common with the surf along the South Shore, and I finally had to quit thinking about home or I knew I'd go crazy.

Wednesday, October 13, 1943—Mr. Ferguson was making out the Watch, Quarter & Station Bill today, which is a chart showing where each man goes at General Quarters, fire, Special Sea Detail (getting underway or landing), steaming watch, collision, man overboard, abandon ship, and so on. He looked over at me and said, "Bowers, you said you're a Signalman striker, didn't you?"

"Yes, *sir*," I replied, firmly. "All the way."

12

"It says in your record you completed the course at the Sound School. What's that all about?"

"Oh, that," I said, my heart sinking. "That was some sort of foulup, sir. I applied for Signal School, and somebody misread my writing."

"To the best of my knowledge there is no Signal School," he said.

"Oh," said I. "Well, I guess that explains it."

"We'll put you down as standby sonarman," he said, making a note.

"But sir," I began, "I mean—"

"We rotate the men on the sound stack," he went on. "The helmsman, the lookouts, and the sound man rotate every half hour. It gives them a little variety. You know anything about guns?"

"A little, sir," I said. "But—"

"Then you'll be a loader for the starboard 20-millimeter at GQ." He made another note.

"What about my signalling, sir?" I asked, plaintively. "When am I going to do that?"

"You can learn that as you go along," he replied. "Then if and when you get rated, we can move you around."

And that's how the big Signalman striker became a sonarman and gun loader.

Thursday, October 14, 1943—I met the leading Signalman today. He's a lean, hawk-nosed First Class who must be anyway thirty-five years old, in recognition of which the guys call him Pappy. He was on the cruiser *Helena* when she was sunk off the Solomons, and, like Linkovitch, he asked for new construction in small ships. His real name is Alvin Nabors, but nobody calls him that. The men call him Pappy, and the officers call him Flags. For some reason, his given name doesn't seem to fit. I asked him if he'd help me with my exam for Signalman, and he asked how fast I could send.

"Oh, maybe six or seven words a minute," I said, trying to sound casual. "I never counted."

"How fast can you receive?"

"I don't know. Not quite so many."

"Well, sonny, you gotta send *and* receive at least eight a minute before you can even start thinking about your crow."

"My—?" I didn't understand.

"Your crow." He pointed to the eagle atop the rating badge on his right arm. "And always remember—never send faster than you can receive."

"Will you help me practice?"

He looked at me queerly. "Just how much signalling *have* you done?" he asked.

"Not a hell of a lot," I replied.

"Like none?"

"More or less."

He smiled. "Maybe it's better that way. At least you got no bad habits I gotta break you of. We'll take it slow and easy, and by damn if we don't make a Signalman outa you."

Suddenly, everything seemed all right. "Thank you, Pappy," I said.

Friday, October 15, 1943—There's another Pacific veteran in our crew, a guy named Lanahan. He was at Pearl Harbor, on the *Tennessee*, and says he shot down a Jap plane with a machine gun. He has the ribbons and the battle star to prove he was there. There's a funny thing about him, though—he's been in the Navy three years and is still a Seaman Second, which to me would mean he doesn't know what he wants to do. I asked him how come he hadn't made a rate, and he shrugged. "You don't need a crow if you know the ropes," he said. "I get everything I want without all the sweat of being a petty officer."

"I never thought of it that way," I said.

"Only suckers go out for a rating," he went on. "And what do you get? You break your butt for a stupid crow, and suddenly you got a lot more work on your hands. Take my advice and relax, and everything will come to you."

The way he said it made it sound logical, but I still think I want to be a Signalman. Maybe I'm being a sucker, but then . . .

Sunday, October 17, 1943—Nothing doing today, so this is as good a time as any to explain about PCs. (I write as though this diary was going to be published . . . well, who knows?) Anyway, during 1942 the German subs sank so many ships off our coast that something had to be done about it, because they were sinking more ships than we were building. So coastal convoys were set up, which was a good idea as far as it went but there weren't enough ships to escort them. Yachts were converted into escorts by putting a gun and some depth charges on them, but that didn't work, so the PC, or Patrol Craft, program was put through on an emergency rush basis. PCs, as I said, are 173 feet (plus eight inches) long, with two 1800-horse-power Diesel engines, and they can make about 18 knots with a following wind. There's a 3-inch-50 gun up forward (that means the diameter of the bore is 3 inches, and the length of the barrel is 50 times 3, or 150 inches), and a 40-mm Bofors gun aft, and then there are three 20-mm Oerlikon guns—one on the flying bridge, and one either side of the signal bridge—which are designed mostly to keep a sub's crew away from their own guns. In addition there are two depth-charge racks in the stern, and either two or four K-guns, which throw depth charges out to the side, the depth charges being made of 300 pounds of cast TNT, which makes one hell of a bang when it goes off. Finally, in the event it should come to hand-to-hand combat with a sub crew, there are some 1903 Springfield .30-calibre rifles, a couple of Thompson submachine guns, and maybe two dozen hand grenades, kept in watertight tins like tennis balls. In spite of all this a PC is not a particularly formidable ship; I once heard the captain say to Mr. Ferguson, "Basically, our job is to sink the sub without making him so sore he comes to the surface. In an even fight, he'd probably kick the - - - - out of us." A comforting thought, that.

Monday, October 18, 1943—Ensign Campbell, the engineer officer, showed up today, fresh from that Diesel school in Ohio. He's thin faced, with a small mouth, and has small eyes set close to the bridge of his nose. He's very fussy about his hair, which is as curly as Shirley Temple's but not so blond. You get the feeling someone once told him he was good-looking, which he isn't. I'll have to ask Pin-Head what he's like to work under. I don't know why, but I don't think I'd like it.

Linkovitch and I are still correcting charts, and it doesn't seem as though we even made a dent in the pile. At this rate, the war could be over and we'd still be sitting here, marking in buoys or crossing them out. Right now I'm working on Charleston Harbor, where we probably won't ever go. At least it's better than being shot at in the Pacific.

Wednesday, October 20, 1943—The 1207 left the yard today, with the crew in their dress blues and all the yard workers waving and tooting whistles. Our ship was moved around to the finishing dock, but it still doesn't look anything like a ship; it's just a lot of steel that feels more like an extension of the dock than anything else.

Friday, October 22, 1943—The last of our officers reported in today. He's Lieut. (jg.) Samuel Taylor, and he's the gunnery officer. He's quiet, and kind of nothing-looking, but maybe it's too early to judge. Incidentally, I get the feeling that Mr. Murray, my officer, and Mr. Campbell, the engineer, don't like each other. It's nothing you can put your finger on, but you feel it when they're in the room together. There's a silent bristling, although they try to cover it up.

Monday, October 25, 1943—Guess what! I got a letter from Diane today! She's the girl I wrote from Key West, whom I'd met with Harry Coffin at the Spa, and I never in a million years thought she'd answer me. It was a good letter, full of lots of funny stuff (Lennie Dalton, for instance, who's only five feet tall, had his hat eaten by a horse while he was trying to make time with Claribelle Lopez on Main Street), and she says she hopes I'll send her a picture of me and the ship. Imagine that—a girl asking *me* for *my* picture! I'll have to ask someone to take one, but it would be best to wait until the ship is a little better looking. If I was to have one taken now, she'd think I worked in a junk yard. I'll write her tonight and tell her I'll have one taken at sea, which will be much more nautical. Everything would be finest kind, if only I could remember what she looks like.

The trees around the school on the hill have all turned now, and you can smell fall all around you. The air is sharp, and the wind kicks up little riffles on the river, and every now and then you see leaves in the gutters. Where they come from I can't imagine, because I haven't seen a tree this side of the river.

Thursday, October 28, 1943—Caulkins, the Yeoman, is here at the office typing up letters, progress reports, and whatnot, and after the officers had left for the day we got him to let us look at their records. It turns out that the captain, whose name is Arthur Block, was a jewelry salesman before the war; he had some small boat experience, and commanded an SC before coming to this ship. Mr. Ferguson, the exec, was a newspaper reporter and had had only temporary duty at sea; Mr. Taylor, the gunnery officer, had been a forest ranger in Tennessee with no seagoing experience; Mr. Campbell, the engineer, was a Yale graduate who'd flunked out of the NROTC; and Mr. Murray, my officer, also went to Yale but had graduated in one of those accelerated programs whereby you do four years' work in three. He'd also done ROTC, and has just turned twenty-one. (I found out, incidentally, that no officer over thirty can serve on a PC; the life is too rugged for the older men. Apparently with the enlisted men age makes no difference.)

All in all, it isn't a group of officers to strike terror in the hearts of the Germans, but I don't guess we're much different from any of the other PCs. We're all known as the Donald Duck Navy, which will give some idea of our warlike capabilities. But, from what I've heard of what happens in the real warships, I'll settle for life on a PC boat.

Friday, October 29, 1943—A funny thing happened when we were leaving the shipyard this afternoon. It was almost dark, and as the truck went up the hill from the river we saw a group of kids around a bonfire. Some of them were wearing ragged costumes, and masks, and I had to think a while before I realized that Sunday night is going to be Halloween. We've been so far removed from all that stuff we might as well be in another world, and the

Halloween trick-or-treating seems as unreal as a kid's birthday party in Siberia. I remember, one night when I was little, I got separated from my brother when we were trick-or-treating, and all I could see were the Jack O'Lanterns of other kids moving about in the darkness. Scared the bejeezis out of me, and in my panic I somehow got lost. What a night.

Monday, November 1, 1943—Still another Pearl Harbor veteran has showed up. His name is Koster and he's a Radioman Third, and in addition to the Pearl Harbor battle ribbon he has a big, red scar down one shin, with the holes where the stitches went making it look like a centipede. Naturally everybody thought it was a shrapnel wound or something, and he didn't do anything to correct that impression until tonight in the barracks, when Pappy took an interest in it.

"That's some wound you got there, mate," Pappy said. "What did it?"

"Uh—shell splinter."

"How come you got no Purple Heart?" Pappy smelled something, and wasn't going to let him off easy.

"It's in the mail," said Koster, looking uncomfortable. "My mail hasn't caught up with me yet."

"It's nearly two years since Pearl Harbor," Pappy reminded him. "What are they sending it by—turtle express? And if that was a shell splinter, how come you still got your leg? I don't think you know what a shell splinter *does*."

Koster cleared his throat. "If you must know, I broke my leg playing softball," he said. "But this is always good for a few free drinks. Sit on a bar stool, pull up the pants leg to show the scar, and pretty soon a civilian is offering to buy drinks. Who's gonna knock that?" He grinned, and Pappy turned away without a word. Nobody said anything to Koster the rest of the evening.

Wednesday, November 3, 1943—The bin where we put our spare parts is almost full, and pretty soon we'll have to start loading them aboard ship. The ship suddenly has begun to look like something, and the whole exterior is painted. They're still working on the inside, however, and when you go aboard the welders' torches look like fat, blue fireflies in a cave. There's the smell of hot steel everywhere, mixed with the smell of fresh paint (the paint, by the way, is what they call fire-retardant, which is next best thing to fire-proof). There's still something missing; I don't know what it is, but the ship has no feeling of its own. It's afloat, and all that, but it's not alive. Maybe I'm being too picky; I don't know.

Got a letter from the folks today, telling me to remember to change my socks if they get wet. Mom is always reminding me of how many colds I had when I was a little kid. I guess she means well, but . . . ah, well. Let it pass. No letter from Alice since Key West.

Thursday, November 4, 1943—Our shipfitter is a round-faced guy from Kentucky named Robbins, and he reminds me a little bit of Burl Ives, the singer. He plays a guitar and likes to go around barefoot. He's cheerful and easygoing, and since his duties aren't too tough (a shipfitter is a combination plumber, welder, and general handyman, who fixes things when they get bent or busted) he's never in much of a sweat. Tonight, back in the barracks, we were talking about what we'd do if we got a week's leave, and most all of us said we'd head straight for home. Robbins said he'd need at least two weeks to make the trip worth while, and when Linkovitch asked him why he said, "Man, to get to where ah come from, you got to swing the last three days on vines." I guess he's exaggerating, but probably not much. At any rate he's happy right here, so long as he's got his guitar. He says he's put on fifteen pounds since he's been in the Navy. Never had such good food in his life, he says. I hate to think what he was eating before, because the chow isn't all that great. When I compare it to what they serve at Cy's Green Coffee Pot, it's so much garbage. Just writing that makes me think of those Friday night suppers at Cy's, after we'd done the week's marketing, when Mom said she was going to enjoy someone else's cooking for a change, and Dad got a slight bun on and kept trying to pinch Leila, the waitress, on the can. It was the same every Friday, and Leila never moved her can out of his reach, so I guess she didn't mind. Mom just pretended she didn't notice. Now I'm homesick again.

Friday, November 5, 1943—Our crew is up to strength now, except for Gunner's Mates. We're supposed to have two, a First and a Third Class, and all we've got is a Third named Lindquist, whose only experience with guns is with a .22 on his uncle's farm in Minnesota. And even that didn't have a front sight, so he never hit anything. We're going to be some warlike bucket, if we've got nobody who knows how to use the guns. The boys who went to the gun school in Newport were all Seaman Firsts (except for Lindquist), and they know as much as any school can teach you in a week—which isn't much. We may have to resort to coffee mugs, like the guys on the *Borie*. (The *Borie*, an old four-pipe destroyer, rammed a sub but didn't sink it, and the sub crew started to come aboard, fighting. The guys with guns were shooting at them, but the 20-millimeters were useless because they wouldn't depress far enough, so everybody threw whatever was handy—coffee mugs, battle

21

lanterns, fire axes, whatnot—until finally the boarders were repelled, and then taken prisoner. I certainly hope we're never put in a spot like that.)

Sunday, November 7, 1943—Lanahan, the guy who's been a Seaman for three years, slipped out last night and went on a good, roaring drunk in Brooklyn. How he got past the sentries, both coming and going, nobody knows; all we know is when we woke up this morning there he was, fully dressed and lying on the deck next to his bunk, the front of him all covered with egg salad sandwich and puke and assorted debris. He had a slight cut over one eye, indicating he'd probably been in a fight, but everything considered he was in pretty good shape. He took a shower, and swabbed off his clothes, and has been acting pleased with himself all day.

Monday, November 8, 1943—There are two colored Steward's Mates in the crew, whose main job is to take care of the officers—serve their food, clean the wardroom, make up their bunks, and so on. The officers eat the same chow we do but they eat it in the wardroom, which is just big enough for all five of them to sit down together provided two of them sit on the transom, which is Navy for couch. They sleep two to a stateroom, in upper and lower bunks like in a Pullman compartment, and they have their own head and shower. We have triple-decker bunks and sleep in two big compartments forward (although the guys who work in the galley sleep in the crew's mess hall, aft), and we have one community head and showers. Green, the senior Steward's Mate, is a big, burly guy who doesn't talk much; there's a rumor he once did time for killing his wife, but I don't see how that can be true because they won't let you in the Navy with a police record. At any rate, he *looks* as though he could have killed his wife, and everyone is careful not to do anything that might rile him up. (Some of the Southern guys find it uncomfortable to be so to speak rubbing elbows with a couple of Negroes, but you can be damn sure they don't say anything in front of Green.) Lincoln, the junior Steward's Mate, is young and kind of plump and happy, and he has two idols—Green and Lena Horne. He keeps a pinup of Lena Horne over his bunk, and he follows around after Green like a puppy. There's talk that the Navy is going to allow colored guys to go out for any rate they want (up till now they've only been allowed to be stewards or messcooks), and Lincoln says he thinks he'll go for Gunner's Mate. Green says he's going to wait and see if it's true before he decides anything.

Friday, November 12, 1943—All this week the yard workers have been doing the final interior work, and suddenly today they took all the hoses, steam lines, electric cables, planking, and tools off the ship, and set about painting the inside. Some of it is painted white and some light green, and in the wheel house the first of the instruments were installed, which should mean we're about ready.

Monday, November 15, 1943—While the yard crew were doing the final touch-up with the paint, we began to load the spare parts aboard. It was an all-day job, and since the majority of the spare parts were for the engine room, a working detail of snipes came over from the barracks to help. They didn't mind the work, though, and I noticed that even Pin-Head Gillis was pitching in with the best of them. This was unusual, because Pin-Head is apt to do what he can to let someone else do the work. It shows what a few weeks in the receiving barracks can do to you.

Tuesday, November 16, 1943—I got talking today with Gibbon, the guy who fell off the catwalk in Fire Fighting

School. He's a Seaman First; his full name is Roy Paul Gibbon, and he comes from Alabama. He's short and mousy, with small eyes and a long, pointed nose, and he does everything very slowly and carefully. He was on a tin can that was cut in two in a collision in the Atlantic, and he, like all the other survivors of sinkings, asked for a small ship. Most of the time he's quiet, but every now and then there's a sort of gleam in his beady eyes that says he's thinking a lot more than he's saying. For all I know he could be laughing all the time, but it only shows in his eyes and not very often at that. He wants to be a Gunner's Mate, because he says back home he could knock a squirrel out of a tree at seventy-five yards. I bit, and asked what kind of gun he used, and he said a flame thrower. Then his eyes lit up like candles, and I knew I'd been had. His Alabama accent is so thick that half the time I don't know what he's saying, so maybe it's happened before. I wouldn't know.

Thursday, November 18, 1943—Today, for the first time, the ship moved under her own power. A yard crew was in charge, since she hasn't been officially accepted by the Navy, and Linkovitch was the only one of us who actually did anything. He had the wheel, and the officers and the rest of us just stood around and watched. The main Diesels turned over with a cough and a roar; blue smoke came out of the exhaust ports in the sides, and when the engines were warm the lines were taken in, and we were off. We went slowly up the Harlem River toward the Hudson, and just as we were about to go under the Spuyten Duyvil railroad bridge Linkovitch's eyes bugged wide and he looked around and said, "The steering's crapped out!" We were heading right toward a bridge abutment, when one of the yard men pulled a knob in the center of the wheel that changed it from power steering to manual, and we eased back into the center of the stream. But it was a hairy few seconds, and the thought of piling a brand-new PC boat into a bridge abutment made us all sweat. We went a few miles up the Hudson, then turned around and came back to the yard dock.

Friday, November 19, 1943—Today we went in the opposite direction, down the Harlem and around into Long Island Sound, where the yard crew tested the engines at various speeds, and checked the time it took from all ahead flank to all back emergency. (With these engines you can't make that jump in one step; you've got to make all the stops along the way—full, standard, two thirds, one third, etc.—and before you go from ahead to astern you've got to stop the engines completely. There ought to be a better way of doing it, but in the PCs at least they haven't discovered it.) Back to the yard again, for all the last-minute items to be brought aboard. I feel like an old salt now, having been twice away from the dock.

Monday, November 22, 1943—Today we left the yard for the last time. We were all standing topside, and as we slid away from the dock a few of the workers waved to us, and we took our hands out of our pockets long enough to wave back. The wind had fangs in it, and since we hadn't drawn our foul-weather gear we were freezing. But the idea of going below never occurred to us; we had to watch everything that happened. The trees around the school across the river had lost their leaves, and the whole landscape looked and smelled of winter, and when we got out in the stream the wind whipped up little bits of spray that every now and then stung our faces like needles. Our 3-inch gun, up forward, was pointing straight in the air (it had been that way when it was installed, and nobody had thought to change it), and for some reason it gave us a more warlike appearance than the situation called for. Groups of boys along the bank cheered and waved at us, but by now we were too cold to wave back. As we went under the various Harlem River bridges they had to open for us (our mast is 55 feet above the water), and I noticed that at one of them a commuter train had been halted. I thought about the people on that train, probably grousing about the lousy railroad service, and it gave me a small smile. This was the first and last time, I thought, that I'd ever have a train wait especially for me. It's a pretty heady idea, if you've nothing else to think about.

We went down the East River to the Navy Yard, and that was the end of feeling important. On the building ways was one of the monstrous new battleships; an aircraft carrier was alongside the drydock, and everywhere you looked destroyers and cruisers were clustered together like cigarettes in a pack. In the midst of all this tonnage a PC looked about as big as a minnow in a school of whales. We sort of crept into our dock, and the yard crew got off and wished us good luck, and that was that.

Thursday, November 25, 1943—Thanksgiving Day, but, more important, our commissioning day. The ceremony was supposed to be held at 11 o'clock—or 1100, as the Navy likes to call it—and the crew had come aboard at 0900. A truck took us from the barracks to the dock, and we carried our sea bags up the gangway and onto the ship, where Mr. Ferguson gave us slips showing where our bunks were and what our various duties would be. (We still haven't got a Gunner's Mate First, so poor Lindquist is the leading gunner.) It was cold—colder even than Monday—and we all stayed below until almost time for the ceremony to begin. Then we formed up on the after deck,

26

with the officers facing us, while the officers' invited guests huddled in the lee of the stack in order to keep from freezing. A Navy band stood on the dock, waiting to play the National Anthem. All that was missing was a Commander Sasse, the Navy Yard officer who was to commission us. We waited, and we waited, while the guests turned blue and the musicians' fingers got stiff, but still no Commander Sasse. Finally, after a half hour had passed and people were about to lose consciousness, the band leader came to Mr. Ferguson and said he had another commissioning, and could wait only five more minutes. So Mr. Ferguson went ashore and made a phone call, and came back to report that Commander Sasse was on his way. It seems our commissioning had slipped his mind. He arrived, and read the orders putting us in commission; the captain, in a clogged voice, read his orders to take command; the band played a honking version of the National Anthem; and then the commissioning pennant, the Union Jack, and the colors were hoisted. I was on the jack, up forward, and my fingers were so numb I caught one of them in the halyard and didn't even know it until I tried to take my hand away. We are now a full-fledged fighting ship of the U.S. Navy.

Friday, November 26, 1943—The first time underway with our own crew. We left the Navy Yard and moved gingerly down to the tip of Manhattan, then through the harbor traffic to the Section Base at Tompkinsville, on Staten Island, where we'll do further outfitting. As we approached the dock the captain was on the bridge wing, and those of us in the wheel house heard him muttering to himself. Mr. Ferguson looked at him and was about to say something, then realized it wasn't the time for small talk. The landing was perfect; the ship came in as gently as a feather, and one touch of reverse on the starboard

27

never made a rate might be that in all the time he'd been in the Navy he'd never been the six months without a court martial that are required for promotion. Lanahan was sober when he left, and seemed a little wistful.

Tuesday, November 30, 1943—Today we went way up the Hudson to the ammunition depot on Iona Island, near West Point, where we loaded ammunition for our guns. For the 3-inch we got star shells, anti-aircraft shells, and the standard high-explosive shells, each one distinguished by a band of color painted on the nose; and for the 40-millimeter we got armor-piercing and also a.a. shells, which come in clips of four and which—the a.a., that is—detonate automatically at 4,000 yards if they don't hit something that detonates them first. The 20-millimeter come in big drums, and detonate only on contact. On the way back downriver we ran into a pea-soup fog, just like the kind at home, so the captain decided to anchor for the night. Someone has to ring the ship's bell at intervals throughout the night, but I kind of like the sound. It reminds me of home, which otherwise would seem thirty thousand miles away.

Wednesday, December 1, 1943—We came back to the Section Base this morning, and guess what. As we nosed toward the pier we saw a garbage detail working right where we were going to land; there were about a half dozen guys manhandling G.I. cans along the stringpiece, and all of them were Negroes except one. That one was Joseph Richard Lanahan, and when he saw us he waved and tried to make it all look like a joke, but you could see he was falling apart inside. Apparently the exec of the Base decided to show the new guys on our ship what happens to smartasses, and I must say he succeeded. Nobody said much of anything while we secured, and when we finally got ashore the garbage detail was gone.

Thursday, December 2, 1943—Went to a small island down the Bay today, and loaded depth charges. We also loaded mousetrap ammo, which I guess I haven't mentioned before. Mousetraps are two racks up in the bow, which throw rocket-propelled explosives out ahead. Unlike the charges, which go off at a pre-set depth, the mousetraps explode only on contact, and they don't roil up the water the way a D/C does. One of them can blow a hole the size of a twelve-year-old boy in a sub's pressure hull, and you fire off a pattern of eight at a time. They also let you keep contact on the sub, whereas in a D/C attack you lose contact before you pass over him, and then have to find him again through all the turbulence caused by the charges. It's a new gizmo, the mousetrap, so nobody's sure if it's good in anything except theory. The theory, so far as it goes, is fine.

Friday, December 3, 1943—Got our orders today, to go to Miami for shakedown. We leave next Monday, so the captain decided to give as many men liberty as possible. He let two sections, or two-thirds of the men, off at a time, one section staying aboard tonight, another tomorrow night, and so on. But the two sections that have liberty Sunday have got to be back by midnight, or there'll be no liberty for *anybody* in Miami.

Monday, December 6, 1943—We shoved off at 0900 today, and the last thing we did before singling up the lines was send a Sailing List, giving the name of every man aboard, over to the Operations Office. This is just a precaution, so if we're sunk they'll know who's aboard and how many people to look for. Everyone got back on time, so there was no problem there. I think Lanahan's disaster has given us all something to think about.

It's a cold, gusty day, and as we threaded our way down

the Bay it was crowded with merchant ships, waiting to make up a convoy. Then we went past the gate ship and out Ambrose Channel, and when we rounded the Ambrose sea buoy and turned south the ship shuddered and kicked up clouds of stinging spray. It's a bleak winter day on the bridge, but below decks everything is warm; the radio is playing ("Pistol-Packin' Momma"), and from the galley comes the smell of cooking food. The ship has finally taken on a life of its own. And if that sounds poetic or sloppy, I'm sorry. That's the way I feel.

II · THE ATLANTIC

Friday, December 10, 1943—Well, there goes the theory
you don't get seasick if you're topside. I'd no sooner finished
writing that last entry than the far end of the mess hall
(where we all write) began to swoop like a gull, and I felt
my stomach swoop with it. I scurried up the ladder and
went to the rail by the starboard K-gun, while my mouth
watered and I felt alternately light and heavy. I took in
great lungfulls of cold air, but with it I also got a lot of salt
spray and Diesel exhaust, so I lurched over to the lee rail
and tried to breathe deeply there. By now the whole world
was swooping, with the horizon first high up and then down
almost out of sight, and the ship was plunging like a
jumping horse, every now and then hitting something solid
that sent sheets of spray high in the air. I think it was the
change from weightlessness to heaviness that finally got
me; my guts didn't know which way was up, and my
stomach finally said the hell with all this, and turned itself
inside out. I puked until there was nothing left to come

up, and then, feeling limp as a string, I sagged back down to the mess hall and lay on one of the benches. I didn't care if I lived or died, and almost hoped it would be the latter.

I'm glad to say I wasn't alone; the mess hall was just what its name sounds like—one big mess. Some guys were able to get topside and some weren't, and the one rule was each man had to clean up after himself. This was only fair, because the quickest way to get seasick is to clean up after someone else. Once it gets started, it's like a brush fire.

My memories of the next three days are blurred. I remember going through the radio shack and seeing Koster, the man with the scar on his shin, wearing headphones and puking into a wastebasket as he typed out an incoming message; I remember Linkovitch, who'd never been on anything smaller than a battleship, blowing lunch for the third time that day because he'd heard the way to cure seasickness was to eat again; I remember the captain, who believe it or not was also sick, standing with Mr. Ferguson on the flying bridge and shouting, "I'm not afraid to die, Mom—I'm not afraid to die!"; I remember Mr. Murray, so sick he could barely stand up, sagging against the bridge wing like a rag doll; and I remember old Gibbon, lying face down on a bench in the mess hall and being hit on the head by a piece of 2 × 4 shoring timber, which came adrift from its rack on the overhead and sailed all the way across the room to skull him. Newman, the Pharmacist's Mate, had to put in six stitches to close the wound.

The worst part of the trip was around Cape Hatteras, off North Carolina, which I hear is always rough no matter what the time of year. Then we cut southwest, past Cape Lookout and Cape Fear (we stayed close inshore, to avoid the north-flowing Gulf Stream), and while it was rough it was nothing like Hatteras, and people began to feel like living again. Then down the South Carolina coast, past Cape Romain and Charleston, and by the time we got to Georgia and then Florida the weather was clear and the sea was calm.

All along the way we saw masts sticking out of the shallow water, showing where merchant ships had been torpedoed, and there were long oil slicks, some of them going for miles, which were from the bunkers of the sunken ships—like dead bodies that were still bleeding.

Saturday, December 11, 1943—We came into Miami today, and I for one felt as though we'd just been around the world. From around Palm Beach southward you couldn't tell there was a war on; big sports fishermen crisscrossed the waters around us, and sometimes they yelled at us when it looked as though we might pass over their lines. I was lookout on the flying bridge, and I heard the captain say to Mr. Ferguson, "I'd like to lob a shell into the beach there, just for good luck."

"Why so?" said Mr. Ferguson, scanning the water ahead with his binoculars.

"Last year, when the subs were sinking everything in sight, West Palm Beach was the only city on the Atlantic seaboard that refused to dim their lights. Said it would be bad for business. The loom of those lights showed for twenty miles, and when you went past you were silhouetted like ducks in a shooting gallery. I'm surprised nobody put a shell in there long ago."

"Do they brown-out now?" asked the exec.

"I don't know. I haven't been down here since."

As we rounded the sea buoy and headed in the Miami channel, the houses on the beach were white and sparkling in the sun. The captain and Mr. Ferguson looked at the scene in silence for a while, then Mr. Ferguson said, "Well —after *that*, what would you like to do?"

The captain thought a moment, then laughed. "I guess have a drink," he said.

Sunday, December 12—I got a rude shock today. All our mail has to be censored by the officers, and we put it in a box which they go over when we get into port. I'd written to the folks, telling them all the interesting things I was putting in my diary, and around noon today Mr. Ferguson called me into the wardroom. He had a pile of letters around him, and mine was in his hands.

"Bowers," he said, "is this true—you keep a diary?"

"Yes, sir," I replied. "My folks gave it to me for my birthday."

"Did you know it's against the rules?"

"Against the—" I swallowed. "How come?"

"Wartime regulations."

"But why?" I saw all my writing time wasted, and with it the chance of writing a book.

"The theory," he said, patiently, "is that, if we should be captured or sunk, and the diary fell into enemy hands, it could reveal secrets we'd just as soon they didn't know."

"But, sir, we're not ever going to be—"

"I'm aware of that. I'm giving you the reason for the rule, and they make no exceptions. Besides, you never know what kind of duty we may draw. PCs are used when they don't want to lose an important ship."

"Oh." This hadn't occurred to me, and it wasn't an especially cheerful thought.

"So I'm afraid I'll have to ask you for the diary," Mr. Ferguson went on.

"What will you do with it, sir?" I asked.

"We'll put it in my safe. That way, in the event of our—

ah—demise"—he gave a wintry smile—"it will be destroyed along with all the other classified documents. If, on the other hand, we survive, it will be returned to you at the end of your tour of duty."

So I gave him the diary, and he thanked me and gave me a receipt for it. I went back to the mess hall, where guys were hurriedly writing letters to get them off in the first mail, and it occurred to me there was no reason I couldn't write my diary in letter form—that is, on writing paper instead of in a book—and stash it away in my locker. I see Mr. Ferguson's point about obeying the law, but there's no possible way we are ever going to be captured, and besides even if I tried I couldn't tell any Navy secrets. A lot of good it would do the Germans to know we have a so-called New England boiled dinner every Thursday which tastes like grasshoppers boiled in dishwater, or that the code flags Fox Negat mean "Disregard My Movements," or that chlorinated water makes absolutely rotten lemonade. That, except for what I learned in Sound School, is about the extent of my Navy knowledge, and I don't see it tipping the scales of war one way or the other. Besides, the letter form doesn't keep me down to one page a day the way the diary does; I can go on as long as I want if it seems worth while.

Sudden thought: Listening to the other guys talk, I've found there are several expressions Nantucketers use all the time that you don't hear anywhere else. "Finest kind," for instance, is strictly a Nantucket expression, and so is the word "some" when it means "very." If I'm going to think about ever being published, I'll have to try and make my language a little more sophistocated (sp?). Not hoity-toity, mind you, just sophistacat . . . ah, the hell with it. Grown up. I wish Miss Gresham was here.

Monday, Dec. 13—We got mail today, and I had four letters! The first was from the folks (I say first because it came out of the bag first), and it was pretty much the usual stuff. The price of scallops is up but you need gas coupons to run the boat; the only decent meat on the Island is at Atchley's and that's black market and costs a bundle; Georgie Lennox (who's not quite five feet tall) had a car fall off a jack onto his head but it didn't hurt him much; Mouse Fenwick was killed in North Africa; and I should remember to change my socks when they get wet. Mouse is the first guy I know who's been killed, and it gave me a funny feeling. Mostly, it made me glad I'm not in the Army.

The next letter was from Miss Gresham, and she gave me the old gung-ho line but at the same time she gave me some good advice, which was that I should pay attention to everything I saw, and try to remember small details, because she was sure that some day I'd be able to write about my experiences. This was almost spooky, coming as it did on top of what happened yesterday, and I decided that Somebody was giving me the old Green Light. (This may be hard to explain to Mr. Ferguson if he ever catches me, but that's a chance I'll have to take. I'm not one to buck Fate when it comes right up and kisses me on the nose.)

The third letter was from Alice, and she used up most of the paper explaining why she'd been so long in writing. First off she'd been laid up with a cold (you'd think that would have been the perfect time to write), then she had a fight with Slappy Souza and was so sore at him she didn't trust herself to talk to anyone else (and *there's* a half-assed excuse if ever I heard one), then she got a part in the Christmas play and is busy studying for that (if it requires virginity, no amount of studying is going to do any good), and so on and so on and so on. I almost didn't finish the letter, and decided I could save myself a lot of time and paper by skipping her the next time I'm in a writing mood.

The last was from Diane, and as usual it was the best. I'd asked her for a picture when I wrote, telling her I'd get one to her as soon as I had a decent one taken, and the picture she sent me, while it doesn't do her justice (or what I remember of her), is still better than nothing. Her face is a little blurry but she's smiling, so what the hell. By trimming off her feet I can fit it in my wallet, and since feet never did anything for me one way or the other this is just right. The important parts show up finest kind. (Find another word for that.) But her letter was the real gas. Apparently the Fire Department is also the Civil Defense unit on the Island, and they recently decided to hold a drill, to practice getting a person out of a burning building. There's an old two-story shack out in the bog, which used to belong to Gus Webster, but it was condemned long since and they figured it would be the perfect thing to burn. So they rounded up Lester Follick and got him to agree to be the person they saved, and at the set time they went out to the bog and waited for Lester to show up. They waited and they waited but there was no Lester, so they finally figured he'd got beered up and gone to sleep somewhere, and since it was getting near noon and time for dinner they decided to set the fire anyway, which they did. Well, in one sense they were right about Lester—he had got beered up and he had gone to sleep, but he was on the second floor of the building, having gone there early so's to be sure to be on time. The flames and the smoke went pouring up and suddenly Lester sticks his head out a window and yells, "Ya gah-damn fools, get me outa here —I'm burning up!" Two of them go tearing into the building and up the stairs, but they're laughing so hard that when they pick Lester up to carry him out they drop him on his head, and he rolls all the way down the stairs, cursing a blue streak. By now the whole Fire Department is laughing so hard they can't aim the hoses straight, so they pack up and go home to dinner, letting the shack burn to the ground itself.

The only tough thing about getting a letter from Diane is trying to think up an answer; nothing has happened so far that can top what she writes about. Well, maybe time will take care of that.

This afternoon I tracked down Doc Newman, the Pharmacist's Mate, and got him to agree to take a picture of me. He's been issued a camera so he can take pictures of any sub we may see, because at GQ his only other job is to sit around the wardroom and wait for someone to get hurt. With any luck, he won't be all that busy. He said he'd take my picture next time he has the camera out.

Wed. Dec. 15—I got a chance today to ask Pin-Head about Mr. Campbell, the engineer officer. Pin-Head looked around, then held his nose and made a motion like pulling a chain. "He's a white-hat," he said.

"What do you mean?"

"Wants to be one of the boys. Just call me Joe—that kind of crap. So when he tries to chew you out, nobody listens."

"So who's in charge?"

"Rinaldi. The Chief's more officer than Campbell will ever be."

I digested this, remembering my first impression of Mr. Campbell, and concluded I'm lucky to have the division officer I do. Mr. Murray is young, and at times an awful eager beaver, but at least he doesn't play buddy-buddy with the enlisted men. And I couldn't ask for a better petty officer than old Pappy, who, just as he promised, is teaching me the ropes slowly but with great care. When Pappy says I'm ready for a crow, I know I will be—there'll be no sweat there.

Dec. 22—This last week has been nothing but drills, drills, and more drills. Base officers from the Submarine Chaser Training Center come along to check us out on how we're doing, and every now and then they throw a problem at us to see how we react. The captain won't be happy until we can get to GQ in one minute flat, with all stations reporting manned and ready. This at first involved a great deal of running around and bumping into one another, but once we got it straight that you go forward and up on the starboard side, and aft and down on the port side, a certain amount of order settled in. It still requires a lot of running, and the last man through a door or hatch has to dog it closed to make the compartment watertight. (In that line, at one GQ drill I saw three guys come squirting out a hatch; the third man slammed it and dogged it tight, then they ran off to their stations. A few seconds later there was a clanging thud, and then slowly the hatch opened and old Gibbon came out, having run full speed up the ladder and rammed his head against the hatch cover. He ran off, tottering a bit, and finally showed up at his station as loader on the port 20-millimeter.)

And, speaking of Gibbon, I overheard something yesterday that set me thinking about him. We'd secured from all drills and were heading back to the Base, and Gibbon was leaning on the lifeline staring at the blue-green water as it sloshed past. There was no wind and he made no quick movement, but suddenly his hat flew off and sailed into the water. He watched it disappear in the wake, then he spat once into the sea and turned and went below. Behind me, I heard the captain laugh.

"So he's one of those," he said.

"One of what?" said Mr. Ferguson.

"A hat loser. Last ship I was on, we had a man who couldn't keep a hat more than three days. Five guys would be standing at the rail, and his would be the one that blew off."

"It didn't seem to bother him much," Mr. Ferguson observed.

"He's probably used to it by now," said the captain. "When you're one of those, you learn not to let the little things upset you."

I thought back on what I knew of Gibbon—his falling in the oil at Fire Fighting School, his getting skulled by the 2 x 4, his running up the ladder into the closed hatch—and it occurred to me he was more than just a hat loser; he was simply a man who was dogged by bad luck. Then I remembered that his other ship had been cut in two, and I wondered if his luck was catching. It was an awful thought, because a PC isn't big enough to take a whole lot of bad luck and still stay afloat.

But old Gibbon hasn't been the only one to get bruised; even the captain got skulled today. And of all days for it to happen, this was probably the worst. The captain and Mr. Ferguson had gone ashore last night and tied on a good snootful for themselves (Caulkins, who had the gangway watch when they came back, said he had to walk behind them and shine his light through their legs so they wouldn't bump into things), and this morning the Base sprung a firing exercise on us. We steamed out toward the firing range, and as we passed the sea buoy the captain called GQ, while the exec held a stopwatch to see how long it took. One of the three 20-millimeter guns is on the flying bridge, directly behind where the captain was standing; when not in use it's left pointing straight in the air, and to cock it you hitch one end of a steel lanyard to the base and the other end to the barrel spring, then slam the barrel down to horizontal, which compresses the spring and cocks the gun. Well, today the captain was standing in the one spot he shouldn't; when the gunner cocked the 20-mm behind him the barrel came down smack on his skull, and almost drove him into the deck like a spike. His dark glasses flew off, his cap developed a permanent crease, and you could almost hear his teeth grind together. It wasn't the gunner's fault, and the captain didn't try to pretend it was; he retrieved his cap and glasses, gingerly felt his scalp and looked at his fingers for blood, then took a deep, shuddering breath.

"All stations manned and ready, sir," said Mr. Taylor, who was wearing headphones, and the exec clicked his stopwatch.

"One minute seven," he said.

The captain said nothing.

The firing exercise itself was sort of fun, if you don't mind a little noise. The drill is, you fire off a couple of clips from the 40-millimeter, which detonate at 4,000 yards and leave little black puffs of smoke in the sky (the tracers, by the way, look like red-hot golf balls drifting around in the air), and then from the 3-inch gun you fire a.a. shells at the smoke, and see how close you can come. The 40-mm makes a surprising amount of noise—it sounds as though someone were using a riveting hammer on your skull—but the 3-inch is the one that really rocks you back.

It's not a big gun but the barrel is fairly short, so the explosion gets to the air that much sooner, and when it goes off there's a flash of bright yellow flame, you're hit in the face by a blast of hot air that's as solid as a mattress, and the ship jumps and the deck plates ring like chimes. I noticed that the captain and the exec got laughing, because with each shot their dark glasses fogged up, and they had to take them off and wipe them. What their heads—especially the captain's—must have felt like, I hate to imagine.

The 20-mm, which is my station, was something of a comedown after all this noise. The gunner is strapped in with a web belt that goes around his back; he aims the gun by moving his body, and the job of the loader (me) is to keep fresh drums of ammunition coming as they're needed. (It's a 60-round magazine, and the gun fires at a rate of 450 a minute, so any prolonged firing can keep you pretty busy. The magazine weighs 63 lbs., which is no feather duster.) What we did was throw a few cartons overboard, then circle away and give them a going-over, but you couldn't see much in all the spray and it was hard to tell how you were doing. So we sent up a flare, which came down slowly by parachute, and when we shot at *that*, we could tell how good our aim was. It was rotten.

When we'd secured from GQ and were headed back for the Base, I saw Doc Newman with his camera, and I asked him to take a picture of me at my gun. Bessinger, the regular gunner, had already gone below to write letters (he writes about five a day, although God knows what he finds to write about), so I strapped myself into the gun and tried to look warlike and pleasant all at the same time. I mean, since it's for Diane I shouldn't be scowling, but at the same time it would look stupid for anyone manning a 20-mm to be all giggles, so I tried to strike a nice balance between seriousness of purpose and the warmer side of my nature. How well I succeeded, we won't know until the picture is developed. I asked the Doc when he'd have it, and he said that depended on when he finished the roll. That, of course, could be a year from next Thursday, so all we can do is hope for the best.

December 26—If anyone should ask me how *not* to spend Christmas, I could tell them in a flash—go to Miami, Florida. Next to Devil's Island, this is probably the most un-Christmassy sinkhole on the face of the earth, and the mere thought of trying to be merry is enough to make you burst into tears. There is, naturally, no snow, and while you can't blame the natives for that you can blame them for making the place look like one big cathouse, which is what they do. Instead of having lots of different colored lights on their Christmas trees they have nothing but red, and you walk through street after street bathed in a dull red glow, which is about as cheerful as a public hanging.

Yesterday—Christmas—was Saturday, so we had one mail in the morning, but most of the Christmas packages had already arrived or were still on the way, and the mail consisted mostly of letters that were mailed so long ago as to have nothing to do with the Holiday Season. I had a package from the folks, which arrived last week but which I saved until today to open, and it was—guess what —two pair of wool socks. There was also a pipe from Diane, but since I've never smoked one it may be a little while before I get the full enjoyment from it. I tried some of Caulkins' tobacco in it, but it was pretty strong and burned my tongue. It also made me feel slightly sick, which is the last thing I need at sea. Still, it was nice of her to think of me, and when I write her I'll have to pretend I've been a pipe smoker all my life.

Caproni, the cook, had done what he could to make a Christmas dinner for sixty-one guys (plus five officers), and while the result was nothing like that you'd get at home it still wasn't bad. And of course compared to the usual Saturday meal of pork and beans, it was elegant. He'd found some tinsel somewhere, which he'd strung up on the overhead, and this I think was a mistake. I'd sooner have no decorations at all than just some ratty tinsel, and I think Caproni felt it too, because he kept apologizing for not having been able to put up grape vines, or fir boughs, or whatever they do in Italy. He also had a Madonna, dangling from a 2 x 4 in the shoring rack, but this did nothing one way or another to the overall effect.

After dinner all but a skeleton crew had liberty, and four of us—Caulkins, Linkovitch, Gibbon, and I—put on our dress whites and went on the town. (Caulkins, by the way, is not like many Yeomen—some of them tend to be on the fruity side, but there's nothing the matter with him. He'd get along in any liberty party.) We wandered around, squinting in the glare of the early afternoon, and the first place we stopped was a stand that sold ice-cold beer in mugs that'd been kept in the freezer, and were all coated with ice. We had a couple of beers apiece and then moved on, and it wasn't long before all that cold had a griping effect on our guts. We made it to the USO canteen, which was full of smoke and guys shooting pool and playing Ping-Pong, and after a while our guts felt better and we started out again, our heads aching from the smoke. We stood on a street corner and looked around, trying to think what to do next.

"If this was Pearl Harbor," said Linkovitch, "I'd know exactly where to go."

"And if it was Loachapoka, Alabama, so would ah," Gibbon replied. "The trouble is, it ain't. It is Miami, Florida, and we is stuck with it."

Caulkins looked thoughtful. "Did you ever see a tree dedicated?" he asked.

We all stared at him. "What kind of tree?" Gibbon asked.

"Any kind. You read about trees being planted, and dedicated to something, but I've never seen it happen."

"Ah don't recall ever having read about it," said Gibbon. "Is it a bang-up affair?"

"I don't know," Caulkins admitted. "That's what I'd like to find out."

"I got a better idea," said Linkovitch. "Let's go someplace dark, where we can think. This sun is baking my brain."

So we went to a bar that was cool and dark, so dark that we felt blind when we first walked in, and had to grope our way to the bar stools. We had a round of beers, and then another, and then Linkovitch spied a jukebox and went over and put some change in it. The machine clicked and whirred, and began to play "Mr. Five by Five."

"This is more like it," he said, sitting down.

"Ah don't know what *you're* thinking about," said Gibbon, "but it ain't one damn bit lak what *ah'm* thinking about."

"Time will tell," Linkovitch replied. "We got till midnight."

"I would still like to see a tree dedicated," said Caulkins. "There are very few people who've seen such a thing."

46

"How do you know?" I asked.

"Look at the pictures in the paper. A handful of people, no more. It's an unusual event."

"Who's going to plant a tree on Christmas?" Linkovitch put in. "Any other day of the year maybe, but for today you can forget it."

Caulkins was quiet. "That's right," he said, at last. "I forgot. This is Christmas, isn't it?"

We had a couple more rounds of beer, and when it seemed as though it must be getting near midnight I peered at the clock over the bar. It showed five twenty-five. "Is that clock right?" I asked the bartender.

"Give or take thirty seconds, it is," he replied. "Why? Has she stood you up?"

"Big joke," said Gibbon. "Remind me to laugh."

"No offense," the bartender replied. "Unless you want to get hard-nosed about it."

Gibbon examined him through beady eyes. "Some Christmas spirit," he said.

Linkovitch had just put "Three Little Fishes" on the jukebox, and when he came back to his stool Gibbon glowered at him.

"Man, don't you got no sense of proportion?" Gibbon asked. "What kind of song is that for the birthday of our Lord?"

Linkovitch giggled. "An' dey twam an' dey twam all ober de dam," he sang.

"Back where ah come from, they'd have you in the stocks for that," Gibbon said. "They'd tar and feather you and string you up from a tree. They'd straddle you on a rail and ride you outa town so hard it'd split your crotch like a willow wand. They'd—"

"O.K., O.K.," said the bartender. "Take it easy."

"Ah am takin' it easy." This was a side of Gibbon I'd never seen, and I listened in astonishment as he went on, "Ah'm just tellin' this blasphemer a thing or two for his own good. Back where ah—"

"An' dey twam an' dey twam all ober de dam," Linkovitch crooned, giggling.

"By damn, you cut that out!" Gibbon slammed his beer glass on the bar so hard it shattered, and he found his hand in a puddle of beer and broken glass. One finger was bleeding, and as he started to put it in his mouth the bartender came around and took him by the arm.

"All right—out!" the bartender said. "All of you, get out!"

"Hey, wait a minute," Gibbon began, but he was already halfway to the door.

"You heard me," the bartender said, hustling him along. "If you can't drink quietly, we don't want you here. And that goes for you, too," he said to Caulkins, who was gaping, wide-eyed, as though he'd just seen a murder. "Bunch of goddam sailors think you can do anything you like—I want no part of you."

As we left the bar, the jukebox was playing "Don't Sit Under the Apple Tree With Anyone Else But Me." The sun was gone and a blue twilight had settled in, but the pavements were still warm.

We wandered about for a while, nobody saying much, while we looked at the red-lighted Christmas trees and heard the quiet rustling of the palms. There was a strange smell in the air, which Caulkins said was eucalyptus, but you could never prove it by me. To me, everything smelled of ripe vegetables, and grass, and heat. It was about as Christmassy as Custer's Last Stand.

I don't know how long we wandered, or exactly where

we went, but we finally found ourselves on a sort of residential street, where the houses had small lawns and, of course, the usual red-lighted Christmas trees. A ground-floor window in one house was open, and we could see a family surrounded by the debris of Christmas. They were listening to one of their number, who was reading from a book, and out of curiosity we tiptoed across the lawn to see if we could hear what was being read. Caulkins was in the lead, with me right behind him, and when we reached the window I realized they were listening to "A Christmas Carol," which Miss Gresham had given us a year ago. (A year? It seems like thirty.) I'd always thought it was pretty long and dull, but these people seemed to be eating it up. Suddenly, without warning, Caulkins put his head in the window, raised one finger, and intoned, "We three kings of Orient are," then ducked back into the darkness. There were screams inside, and a certain amount of thrashing about, and we figured we'd better get out of there while the getting was good. We ran to the end of the block, then turned the corner and slowed down. Caulkins was chortling; Linkovitch and I were laughing out loud, and only old Gibbon was silent.

We'd gone maybe three blocks when a glow in the street warned of headlights behind us, and turning around I saw the unmistakable, close-together lights of a jeep. This could mean only one thing—Shore Patrol. "Look out!" I shouted, and we scattered like a covey of quail. Caulkins and I went in one direction and Linkovitch in another, and when I glanced back I saw that Gibbon was still drifting along, as calmly as though he were walking a dog. "Gib!" I yelled. "Shore Patrol!"

"Ah didn't do nothin'," he replied. "Ah got no cause to run."

Then the jeep was alongside him, and the SPs jumped out, and Caulkins and I took off through the bushes. We could hear the SPs crashing around trying to find us, but after a while they gave up, and we stayed in hiding a full half hour before heading back toward the Base.

It was a seedy-looking crew that flopped around the mess hall this morning. Nobody seemed to have had a good time, and the general feeling was a mixture of remorse, irritability, and frustration. Robbins, the Shipfitter, tried to pluck a few chords on his guitar, but someone threw a shoe at him, so he went topside and sat on the depth-charge racks, where anything thrown at him would go over the side. Gibbon was missing, and we figured the SPs had probably put him in the jug for the night, which, considering the fact he'd done nothing, could only be called an example of his luck. Some of the guys tried to write Christmas thank-you notes, but you could see their hearts weren't in it, and they were looking for any excuse to do something else. Lindquist, our lonely Gunner's Mate, has been restricted to the ship for medical reasons for the last week or so, and he was the only one with an even partway clear head. He'd written four or five letters and then come to a block, because he stared at the overhead for a long time before speaking. Finally he turned to Caulkins.

"Hey, Cork," he said. "You're a intellectual. What's the polite word for clap?"

"I don't know," Caulkins replied. "How about social disease?"

Lindquist considered this, then shook his head. "Too hoity-toity," he said. "It sounds like I'd been going to debutante parties and all that la-di-da."

"Then how about gonorrhea?"

"Spell it."

"Uh—g-o-n-o-r . . . I'd have to look it up."

"Forget it. I got the answer." Lindquist scribbled off a sentence, his tongue moving with each letter, and slid it across to Caulkins. "See how that sounds," he said.

Caulkins took the sheet of lined paper, and read: "Dear Aunt Grace, thank you very much for the necktie—"

"Not that part, dummy," Lindquist cut in. "The last part."

"Sorry." Caulkins looked at the bottom of the letter, and read, "I went over on the beach a few nights ago and I guess I bit off more than I could chew, because now I'm restricted to the ship." He put the letter down, and with an absolutely straight face said, "Yes, I'd say that does it."

"I mean, it gets the idea across without being too—what's the word?—florid?"

"Lurid," said Caulkins.

"That's right. Lurid." Lindquist took the letter back, read it with satisfaction, and signed it. "I should of been a writer," he said, addressing the envelope.

Gibbon showed up in time for the noonday meal. He had a small cut over one eye and his upper lip was swollen, and he was once again the quiet, mousy person I'd first known.

"What did they do to you?" I asked.

"Beat me up." He sat down slowly, as though all his bones hurt.

"Why? You hadn't done anything."

He shrugged. "Try and tell them that."

"God damn, I'm sorry," said Caulkins. "This is my fault."

Gibbon shrugged again. "No, it ain't. Ah shoulda run with the rest of you. Ah just didn't think they could be such bastards."

"Did they charge you with anything?"

"Drunk and disorderly. They gonna send the charges to the Old Man, and he gotta endorse it with what punishment he give me."

"Well, we'll soon see to that." Caulkins sounded as though he personally was going to take charge of things. A wispy smile crossed Gibbon's face.

"Don't be too hard on him, Cork," he said. "He got bigger things to worry about than me."

Monday, Dec. 27—A messenger from the Commandant's Office showed up today, bringing the charges against Gibbon and the slip for the captain to endorse with the punishment. The captain called Gibbon into the wardroom, and since Caulkins, as Yeoman, had to take down the proceedings, he was there also. Linkovitch and I volunteered as witnesses, but the captain said he'd call us only if he needed us. We stayed just outside the wardroom door, where we could hear what went on. The captain read the charge and asked Gibbon how he pleaded, and when Gibbon said, "Guilty, sir," Caulkins cut in and asked to be heard. He told the whole story, and when he was through there was a short silence.

"You mean that's all you did?" the captain asked, at last.

"That's right, sir," Caulkins replied. "I was the one who said it, and Gibbon didn't even think it was funny. His only mistake was he didn't run."

There was another silence. "All right," the captain said. "Gibbon, you do wheel, stack, and lookout, don't you?"

"Yes, sir," Gibbon replied.

"Very well. You are hereby relieved of two hundred hours' duty on wheel, stack, and lookout. . . . And as punishment I am giving you two hundred hours' extra duty on the wheel, stack, and lookout. Is that clear?"

"Yes, *sir*," said Gibbon.

To Caulkins, the captain said, "Write on the endorsement that I gave this man two hundred hours' extra duty."

"Yes, sir," said Caulkins. "And his record?"

"Forget about his record. As far as I'm concerned this never happened."

Gibbon's eyes looked like two little fireflies as he came out of the wardroom. "Now there," he said, putting on his new white hat, "is a man ah would gladly die for."

Wednesday, Dec. 29—We had night exercises with some PT boats last night, and I must say it was kind of fun. They went out ahead of us, and the idea was for them to try to get close enough to us for a make-believe torpedo run, while we used our searchlight for make-believe gunfire. They would lay a smokescreen and hide behind it, hoping to surprise us as we came around the end of the line of smoke. Our captain decided on a tricky maneuver, which almost worked too well: instead of going around the screen he cut straight through it, and we came out within a matter of feet of a PT boat that had been laying for us. We gave him a good going-over with our light, which if it had been the real thing would have wiped him out, but when we thought about it later we realized that if we hadn't come out exactly where we did we might have rammed him, in which case there would have been some casualties we hadn't intended. All we can hope is he learned something from it, and if he ever has to lay a smokescreen in the Pacific he'll remember the PC that almost cut him down. You feel funny working with someone who's headed for the Pacific, because that's where there's no fooling around. Guys like Linkovitch and Pappy, who've been through it, are somehow different from the rest of us—I can't say exactly why, but I know it's there.

By the way, I've found out what it is that makes a ship feel alive. It's the blowers—the ventilation ducts—and they are the same to a ship as breathing is to a person. During this morning's drills we went to abandon ship stations (the captain has a theory that if you do it in drills you won't have to do it for real), and with the engines stopped and all the power off, the ship just wallowed in the swells like a dead fish. We launched a liferaft to make sure it would float (sometimes they sink like a brick, which is a poor thing in an emergency), then hauled it back aboard, and after that we secured from the drill. The minute the blowers were started the ship came to life again, and it was almost as though she was giving a sigh of relief. It's funny how close you get to a ship, once you've been aboard a while.

Sunday, Jan. 2, 1944—New Year's around here is pretty much like Christmas—zilch. It occurred to me that I might give the folks a call, but the same thought had apparently occurred to seven million eight hundred and fifty-two thousand other people, and the operator said it would be tomorrow at the earliest before I could get a call through (this was all yesterday). So I went back to the ship and wrote Diane, telling her I'd had my picture taken and would send her a copy as soon as it was developed. After that I looked up Gibbon, who was lying in his sack (the top one in a tier of three), and asked him if he had any bright ideas. He put down his comic book, and looked at me.

"Yeah," he said. "Call off the war, and go home."

Lincoln, the junior Steward's Mate, came through the door from the officers' quarters. "I hear we going to New York," he said. (He keeps his pinup of Lena Horne in the officers' pantry, off the wardroom, and spends as much time there as possible.)

"Where'd you hear that?" Gibbon asked him.

"I just hear the captain and Mr. Ferguson talking about it. We got orders to Staten Island."

"Hot damn," said Bessinger, from his sack across the room. "That means we get the milk run." Bessinger, my partner on the starboard 20-mm, comes from Brooklyn and is never happier than when he's within striking distance of Ebbets Field, no matter whether it's the baseball season or not.

"What's the milk run?" Lincoln asked.

"New York to Key West. Ten days down, a week coming back. A week or ten days in port, then off on another convoy. It's a piece of cake."

"What about subs?"

Bessinger made a rude noise with his mouth, and rolled over.

(It being New Year's Day, the captain had said we could keep our bunks down all day. Normally, in port, they're all made and triced up by 0730. At sea, of course, you get what sleep you can when you can.)

Wed. Jan. 5—We left Miami this morning, and headed north. It's over a thousand miles to New York, and the northbound Gulf Stream gives us a goose of three or four knots, so if we make good speed and the weather holds out, we could get there in a little over three days. I never thought New York would seem like home, but it sure does now. I can hardly wait.

Sun. Jan. 9—Well, we didn't make it in a little over

three days—in fact, we're not there yet. Just south of Hatteras the weather turned sour, and we had to pull down the speed to something like eight knots (we'd been making fifteen). All the topside watches had to wear foul-weather gear, which consists of long johns (if you have them), things like ski pants and a zip-up jacket, oilskins over that, a bath towel around your neck, galoshes on your feet, as many gloves as you can wear, and on your head either a sou'wester or a wool-lined aviator's helmet. Some people like a face mask as well, but I found the wool lining made me sneeze, so I had to do without. The lookout watch on the flying bridge is like having icewater squirted at you from a fire hose, and the idea of trying to see anything at night is just crazy. Still, you have to do it. When you get below you like as not find your gloves have iced up, so you have to beat them on the radiator to thaw them out. The officers wear the same rig we do, only they have sheepskin coats. The main difference there is that their collars, being bigger than ours, tend to funnel more water down their necks.

Then this afternoon, just as we were nearing Ambrose Channel, we got a message from Eastern Sea Frontier, telling us to stand by to receive survivors of a torpedoing. Apparently a merchant ship picked them up to the north of here, but since he's headed for Charleston he doesn't want to go through all the hassle of coming into New York, and asked that someone be sent out to take them off his hands. We, being the nearest ship in the area, have been elected.

We're now patrolling outside the minefield (we hope), waiting for him to show up.

Mon. Jan. 10—He showed up, all right—just before midnight. We'd begun to wonder if we'd got the message right when suddenly this shape loomed up out of the darkness, and then he turned on his running lights and we went alongside. Both ships had to keep moving so as to have steerage way, and it was a tricky maneuver to get close enough to him without actually hitting him. But the captain managed it with no sweat, and then they let down a ladder while we kept our lights on them, and the men began to come down. There were five of them, and they were still pretty much in shock. They'd been given fresh clothes and had cleaned up a little, but there were still traces of oil in their hair, and two of them couldn't stop trembling. We took them down to the mess hall and gave them hot coffee and blankets, and when I went topside again I saw a wire stretcher being let down onto our deck. It was a rig called a Stokes basket, and it was formed in the shape of a man with straps to hold him in, but the figure in it was completely wrapped in a blanket, head and all, and it took me a couple of seconds to realize he was dead. There's a work-light on our stack, which illuminates the entire after part of the ship, and the way it lit up the blanket-wrapped figure was—to say the least for it—spooky. It was as though you were hypnotized, and I found myself staring at it and waiting for it to move. But it didn't; it was the stillest thing I'd ever seen. Mr. Ferguson came back aft, and Van Gelder, the Bosun's Mate First who was in charge of the detail, asked him where to put it. Everyone was standing around, not knowing quite what to do.

"Put him over by the stack, there," Mr. Ferguson said. "As far out of sight as you can."

Van Gelder and a couple of seamen did as directed, then the work-light was turned off, and we veered away from the merchant ship and headed in the channel. Nobody said much for the next hour or so.

An ambulance was waiting at the pier when we docked, and the five survivors climbed aboard. There was some trouble fitting the Stokes basket in after them, but it finally got wedged in so the back door would close, and the ambulance drove slowly away. It was after two by the time we hit the sack.

Mon. Jan. 17—We started off on our first convoy today. At 0400 we were routed out of our sacks; we had coffee and rolls in the mess hall, then went to Special Sea Details. The last thing before we singled up the lines was the sailing list; Caulkins had made duplicate copies of our roster, one of which went to the Operations Office and one to the PC 1171, which is to sail with us. In return we got the 1171's sailing list, and with that we singled up the lines, cast off, and snaked our way into the stream. Everywhere you looked there were lights; some were blinking, and they were buoys, but there were also lights on the beach and lights on the ships at anchor, and it was practically impossible to tell one from the other. It was like being shut in a closet with a million fireflies, and having to pick your way between them without touching one. Somehow the captain managed it; he got a fix on the blinking green light off Fort Wadsworth, in southern Staten Island, and then he found the gate ship, and finally we were going out Ambrose Channel. It was cold, and an icy mist came in from the sea, but I found I was sweating when we cleared the harbor. What the captain felt like I can't imagine, but he looked as though he'd been doing it all his life. It was hard to believe that a couple of years ago he was selling jewelry.

It was just getting light when we cleared the channel, and we patrolled back and forth while the merchant ships came out and formed into the convoy. There were fourteen ships and three escorts; we had the starboard beam of the convoy, the 1171 had the port beam, and the escort commander, an old four-pipe destroyer named the *Broome*, was dead ahead. The ships formed into columns, and each ship had a number: the third ship in the first column, for instance, would be number 13; the fourth ship in the third column 34, and so on, so the setup looked like this:

11	21	31	41
12	22	32	42
13	23	33	43
	24	34	

That is, that's the way it was supposed to be, and that's the way it looked at the beginning. Later on, you couldn't describe the way it looked except to say it was a mess.

The convoy speed was eight knots, but we hadn't been going for more than an hour when it was clear that ship 34 couldn't make the speed. Either that or he didn't want to; whatever the reason, he began to drop behind, and after a while the *Broome* blinked over to us and told us to find out the problem. After some trouble we raised their signalman, and Pappy sent: "Convoy speed 8 knots pls try conform." Back came the reply: "Engine trouble cannot make speed." We relayed this to the *Broome*, who came back with: "Tell him he either makes speed or will be detached." This was passed along, and in a couple of minutes there was a burst of smoke from the merchantman's stack, and he began to pick up speed.

"Oh-ho," the captain said. "He just wanted an escort all his own."

We resumed our convoy station, and as we patrolled back and forth we saw occasional masts sticking out of the water, and I thought of the survivors we'd picked up the week before. They say the Merchant Marine people make good money, but it would take a lot more than money to make me sail on a ship all loaded down with oil, or explosives, or whatever. But then they probably don't envy us, so I imagine whatever you're doing you can always think of someone who's worse off than you are. I don't know who the infantry guys can feel sorry for, but there must be someone. Flyers, I guess. I once heard a guy say he'd never join the Navy because when the enemy started shooting he wanted someplace he could run to, and on a ship you could only run around the deck. Still, we get hot food and a dry sack, and that makes up for a great deal. There's not much point being able to run if you get to sleep in a mud puddle when you stop. I suppose this sort of reasoning could go on forever.

Jan. 18—Today, by a miracle, the weather was fine. It was one of those clear winter days when the sky is blue and the water even bluer, and the whitecaps look like diamonds in the sun. A blimp from the Air Station in New Jersey came out and patrolled a few miles ahead of us, and this made us feel good because he could keep an eye out for any subs that might be waiting in our track. He drifted around there most of the day, and we finally got so used to him we didn't even notice. He was like a small, fat cloud that stayed always the same distance away. Then, around the middle of the afternoon watch, one of the lookouts sang out "Flare from the blimp!" and we looked and saw a thick column of dirty red smoke dropping down to the surface of the water. The captain said, "Sound General Quarters!" and the Klaxon alarm honked throughout the ship while guys started running to their stations. We were manned and ready in one minute flat, although Bessinger was still trying to get his strap around him while I clipped the magazine in place. This was our first GQ for real, and as I looked around I could tell how the various guys were reacting. Old Gibbon, on the port 20-mm, showed no emotion at all, but Lincoln, the Steward's Mate who was loader on the flying-bridge 20-mm (the one that had skulled the captain) was so nervous he could barely fit his magazine into the slot. Green, the senior Steward's Mate, was talker on the depth-charge racks, and looking back I saw him clearing his phone wire from beneath his feet as he went to the rail and peered ahead. You got the feeling he was ready to throw the depth charges by hand if the release didn't work. Pappy, of course, had been among the first to reach his station; his shoes were untied and his shirttail was hanging out, but he was there at his signal light before some of the guys had even left the mess hall. Mr. Taylor, on the bridge beside the captain, just looked drowsy. As for me, I didn't feel much of anything; I was excited but not scared, and my only thought was what would happen next.

Ahead of us, the *Broome* had put on full speed to go out and investigate the contact, and the 1171 and we slid up from the beams and covered the bow sections of the convoy. We watched the *Broome* nose around in the distance, like a dog sniffing the ground, and then suddenly, off to port, we heard the rattle of gunfire. Bright orange tracers were streaking from the bridge of the 1171, and they kicked up a cloud of spray that completely obscured whatever the target was. The captain ordered our guns to train toward where the 1171 was firing, and then in a very quiet voice he said, "Gun One stand by."

Mr. Taylor relayed this through his headphone, and I heard a click and a metallic thud as a shell slid into the breech. "Gun One standing by," said Mr. Taylor.

"Very well," said the captain, and there was silence. The

1171 had stopped firing, and without turning around the captain said to Pappy, "Ask him what target."

Pappy took the port signal light and clattered out the message, and in a moment the reply came back. I could read it as it came: "Thought it mine now looks like buoy." Pappy relayed this to the captain, who sighed.

"Gun One unload," he said.

There came the click and thud as the breech was opened, and the shell was taken out and put back in the ready ammunition locker. I had a distinct feeling of letdown.

"Signals on the *Broome*," said one of the lookouts, and Pappy sent out a K, meaning go ahead. A single word flashed from the *Broome*'s light, and Pappy gave the R that meant he had it.

"Wreck," he said, disgustedly, and switched off his light.

The *Broome* was heading for the convoy, and the 1171 and we dropped back toward our stations. "Secure from General Quarters," the captain said, and then, to Mr. Taylor, "We'll never get our Navy Crosses this way."

"That's all right with me," said Mr. Taylor, coiling up the wire on his headset. "I'd sooner have a good nap than a Navy Cross any day."

The steaming watch took over, and the men on the off-duty sections went back to what they'd been doing. I drifted down to the mess hall for a cup of coffee, then brought it back up to the depth-charge racks, where Robbins, the Shipfitter, was plucking on his guitar. He looked toward the setting sun, which silhouetted the Jersey shore and touched the edges of the low-lying clouds with fire, and he strummed a few chords and slowly built them into a tune. It was a quiet, gentle melody with no words, and he continued to stare at the shoreline as he played. Then, as though he'd been thinking about it all along, he spoke.

"I wonder what the poor people are doing today," he said.

Jan. 24—We're back in the good weather now, but for a while there I wasn't sure we were going to make it. Just south of Hatteras we ran into the usual heavy seas, and the nighttime visibility was just about zilch. When you stood lookout watch, on the flying bridge, you were ducking the seas that came up and over the ship; in the wheel house, all you could see were the little phosphorescent bugs that covered the ports as the water ran off; and the sonar head was out of water so much that the pinging was all but useless. Add to that the fact that there was so much "sea-return" on the radar—that is, the nearby waves blurred the radar reception—that we might just as well have been blindfolded. But at least you were warm when you had the wheel and the sound-stack watches, and you almost had time to dry off before going topside for lookout duty again (we rotated every half hour). Mr. Murray had the mid-watch—from midnight to 0400—and he was one of the few who hadn't got used to the sea. He was as sick as he'd been the first time out, and it was a wonder to me he could even stand. At one point, when I was on the wheel, I noticed a flash of blue light out forward, and at first I thought it was lightning. Then it came again, and once more, and I realized it was something on the ship that was flashing. I called it to Mr. Murray's attention, and when he saw it he turned to Linkovitch, who was quartermaster of the watch.

"Call the captain," he said, and Linkovitch said, "Aye," and disappeared.

The captain slept in the wardroom underway, so as to be handy to the bridge, and it wasn't thirty seconds before he appeared. He studied the flashing for a while, then said, "There's a loose wire out there. Who's the electrician on watch?"

"Napier, sir," said Linkovitch. "He's on the ready gun."

"Get him up here," said the captain, and Linkovitch was gone again. "It looks like the light on the ammunition locker," the captain went on, to Mr. Murray. "The seas tore it loose."

"Great," said Mr. Murray, as though it were a personal affront. "That's all I need."

Napier appeared, and the captain explained the situation. Napier was an Electrician's Mate Third; he'd been a bartender before the war, and was looking for a trade where he could get life insurance at a reasonable rate. Bartenders and firemen, he'd told us, were all but uninsurable. Now he studied the problem, nodded, and left the wheel house. He reappeared on the foredeck, and we could just barely see him, crawling forward on his hands and knees. He was wearing his kapok life jacket, and had a line around his waist that was secured to a stanchion, but even with all those precautions his job was a risky one. The ship was lurching and bucking; if a wave had swept him overboard it's unlikely his lifeline would have held, and in those seas it would have been impossible to find him. He inched his way forward, and while we couldn't see what he did we saw that the flashing stopped, and then slowly he made his way back aft again.

A lookout's voice echoed through the voice tube from the flying bridge. "It looks like a ship's been torpedoed," he said.

The captain tried to see through the side porthole but his vision was blurred by phosphorescent bugs, so he wrenched the door open and stepped out onto the bridge wing, just in time to be hit by a solid wall of water. He fell back, slammed the door, and shouted up the speaking tube. "Where is it?" he called. "Give me a bearing!"

Before the lookout could answer, a man put his head through the door from the radio room. "Fire in A Compartment," he said.

"One thing at a time," said the captain, and he reached over and pulled the red knob on the GQ alarm. The raucous honking sounded throughout the ship, and over it came the pounding of running feet. "Sound fire alarm forward," the captain went on.

Linkovitch relieved me of the wheel, and said, "Your station's near the bell—you sound it."

The fire alarm was a rapid ringing of the ship's bell, plus one ring for forward, two for midships, and three for aft, and the bell was on the signal bridge, near the base of the mast. As I clawed my way up to the bridge I thought back on the Fire Fighting School, and told myself not to panic. There had been an immediate instinct to jump over the side when fire was first announced, but now I felt somewhat calmer, and I knew no blaze could be as big as those we'd gone through at school. I rang the bell for all I was worth, at the same time looking to see if I could spot the torpedoed ship. I could see vague shapes in the darkness, and while there seemed to be a smudge of smoke off to port there was no sign of an explosion. All around me men were scurrying to their GQ stations, and I saw old Gibbon, carrying a magazine for the port 20-mm, get hit square on the head as his gunner slammed the barrel down to cock it. It knocked him flat on his face on the deck, and he lay there a second, said, "Chrahst," then picked himself up, retrieved the magazine, and snapped it into place.

We stayed at our GQ stations, getting wetter every minute, until finally the word came to secure. The damage

control party had put out the fire, which was in the wiring
—apparently caused by the shorting wire that Napier had
disconnected—and as for the so-called torpedoed ship, there
were no distress calls and nothing on the voice radio, so it
was simply a false alarm. I know from experience a lookout
can see almost anything he wants to at night—the rising
moon, for instance, is often reported as a fire, and a low-
lying star can be taken for a flare—so this guy (my gun-
mate Bessinger, as it turned out) had mistaken a cloud of
stack gas for a torpedo explosion. No great harm was
done, except to old Gibbon's head.

Next morning the sea was no calmer, and the convoy
was all over the lot. Our original straggler, ship 34, was
nowhere to be seen, and the others were scattered, some in
groups and others singly, like a flock of chickens in a high
wind. It took us the better part of the day to herd them
back into any kind of order, and then at night they drifted
apart again. Once or twice we saw smoke on the horizon,
which might or might not have been 34 trying to catch up,
but the *Broome* decided we had enough on our hands without adding one more headache.

Jan. 27—The water down along the Keys is clear and
green, and you get the feeling that the bottom is only
a few feet away. The ping of the sonar seems to echo and
shimmer all around the ship, and it's hard to believe there
could be a sub down there. But then every now and then
you see a mast sticking out of the water, and you know it's
not all that peaceful. My first look at the Keys reminded
me of a pirate book I read when I was a little kid, and the
white sand and the palm trees and the green water all
made me think of the Spanish Main. Then we came in the
Key West channel, through the minefield, and in the drydock I saw a merchant ship with holes from a sub's deck

gun in its superstructure, and I knew the pirates were still here. The sea and the sky and the sand are just as they were in Captain Kidd's time, but now the ships have steel hulls, and the pirates are under the water instead of on the surface. I didn't have this feeling when I was here at the Sound School; it's only coming in from the sea that you're aware of how little has changed in the last couple of hundred years. In my pirate book there was a picture of a man marooned on Dry Tortugas, left there to die for some offense or other, and it gave me a funny feeling to look at our chart and see Dry Tortugas right there, a big sand spit off to the west of Key West. There's a light there now, but aside from that nothing is very different.

Jan. 28—We got into Key West last night, after handing the convoy over to another group of escorts. The first thing we did was go to the fuel dock, then to our berth at Craig Docks, and then all the officers except Mr. Taylor, who had the duty, lit out for the Officers' Club, and the liberty sections of the crew made for the center of town. It doesn't matter how dumpy the place is, any town looks beautiful when you've been to sea for a while, and Duval Street in Key West might just as well have been the corner of Broadway and Forty-second Street. Returning to the ship was trickier than leaving it, because we were nested outboard of another PC and that meant climbing between the ships and over the lifelines. But only two people fell in the water: Gibbon (naturally) and Mr. Campbell. Gibbon took it completely in stride, but with Mr. Campbell you'd have thought it was a dirty trick God had thought up just to plague him. He screamed and cursed and carried on, and when we finally fished him out of the water he didn't say thank you or anything; he just stamped down to his cabin with his shoes making squilching noises, leaving a trail of water behind him. Pin-Head had been one of those standing by, and I noticed that he did nothing to help. I caught his eye as Mr. Campbell disappeared, and he grinned, gave me a thumbs-up gesture, and went back aft.

Jan. 29—We're headed north again, having formed up our convoy in the Straits of Florida. The wind is from the north, and since the Gulf Stream flows northward the opposing wind and tide make a hellish chop on the water, and the PCs are leaping around like salmon. (I may not be able to write too long if it keeps up.) Koster, our Radioman with the scar on his shin, tried to convince Doc Newman he had appendicitis in Key West, but he got screwed up on which side it should be and told the Doc it was his left side that hurt. The Doc gave him some horrible tasting gluck and told him he'd be all right, so here he is still aboard, puking into the wastebasket as he types out his radio messages. You'd think if he was going to fake an appendicitis he'd at least learn a little something about it, but no—he was so eager to stay ashore he said the first thing that came into his head. I'm used to the motion by now, so I don't get seasick unless . . . more later.

Feb. 2—I don't ever want another night like last night. I was on the sound stack just after supper, and the captain came into the wheel house and said to Mr. Murray, "We seem to have a submarine up ahead of us."

I couldn't see Mr. Murray's face, but I could hear the change in his voice as he said, "What do you mean?" He'd been seasick as usual, and his throat was raw from puking, but now a new note crept in, making him sound almost squeaky.

"It came over the radio," the captain replied. "He's on patrol just south of Hatteras."

Nobody said anything for several moments. I don't know

why, but the idea of a submarine was much more terrifying than if we'd actually seen one ahead of us. As it was, we could imagine him lurking there, lining us up in his periscope and maybe accompanied by a whole wolf pack of other subs, and being unable to see him gave the whole thing a spooky quality that made your knees go limp. It occurred to me that, if I'd waited for the Draft to get me, I'd still be safe on Nantucket, without a worry beyond what I was going to do on Saturday night. Darkness had fallen, but there was a huge, towering mass of clouds ahead of us that made the darkness all the blacker, and if you let your mind linger on it you could believe you were sailing over the rim of the earth and into the mouth of hell. (I could understand, incidentally, how the old-time sailors believed it possible to sail off the earth; all you need is a large cloud in the night, and you feel you're about to be swallowed up.)

"Keep a sharp watch on the stack, there," the captain said to me, and I said, "Aye, sir," and bent over the dial as though by sheer concentration I could pick out an echo the sonar beam had missed. There's no mistaking a true echo when you hear one; instead of making a long, wavering, chime-like noise, the signal starts out as always and then suddenly—*ting!*—it's as though someone had jammed a needle in your ear. If the echo is of higher pitch than the outgoing signal it means the target is coming toward you; if it's lower it's going away, and if it's the same pitch it means it's either a beam-on shot or you're pinging on some stationary object, like a wreck. This is known as the Doppler effect, and it's a big help in plotting the course of your target. They say the British can run an attack using nothing but Doppler, but they've been in this business a lot longer than we have.

At any rate, I trained the beam back and forth across the bows, listening so hard I could swear I heard a fish swallow, but there was no hard echo. There was an occasional mushy sound, which could have been the wake of another ship, and once or twice I heard porpoises grunting as they came near us, but if there was a sub out there he was made of sponge rubber, because there was no echo I could hear. Then it came my turn to go on lookout, and I spent the next half hour on the flying bridge, staring into the blackness and trying to keep my binocular lenses dry. I might as well have been blindfolded.

Finally my watch was over, and I went back to the mess hall for a cup of coffee. I had a feeling I wasn't going to sleep much, no matter what, so I figured coffee would be the best thing to help me keep alert. Some guys were writing letters and some were just beating their gums, and as I sat down with my coffee Bessinger was saying, ". . . right to the goddam bottom. Not a goddam person survived."

"Yes, they did," said Napier. "They weren't all lost."

"The goddam depth charges went off," Bessinger said. "Who's gonna survive a thing like that?"

"What's this?" I asked. "What happened?"

"The *St. Augustine*," Bessinger told me. "A converted yacht. She was supposed to rendezvous with a freighter, so when she got it on radar she steered straight for it, and damn if she didn't run smack into it. Went down with all hands."

"She did not," Napier insisted. "There were at least a dozen survivors."

"Who's gonna survive the depth charges going off?" Bessinger demanded. "They'd have been split apart like so many goddam haddock."

"You know the first rule if you're in the water when charges are going off?" Caulkins asked.

"What?" said Bessinger. "Make out your will?"

"Get out of the water," Caulkins replied.

Bessinger eyed him sourly. "Some joke," he said.

"I mean it," Caulkins said. "I read it in the book. 'Rule Number One: Get out of the water.'"

"Then what?" said Bessinger. "Learn to fly?"

"'If this proves impossible,'" Caulkins quoted, "'then raise the thorax so as much of your chest as possible is above the surface, at the same time—'"

"Ah don't got no thorax," Gibbon put in. "Mahn was taken out when ah was a little shaver."

"I still say the *Augie* went down with all hands," said Bessinger. "Unless their charges were set on safe, they had to go off."

"How are our charges set?" Napier asked. "Just out of curiosity, understand."

"We set up for a shallow pattern," said Green, the Steward's Mate who was on the charges at GQ. "The first seven are set at fifty and a hundred, and the rest on safe."

"Great," said Napier. "Then if—" He was interrupted by the General Quarters Klaxon, which shattered the air around us. We looked at each other, wide eyed, and then started running. The darkness topside was complete, and as I climbed toward the signal bridge I could see nothing, but I could hear the rushing swish of the ship's wake, mixed with the thud of running feet and the clatter of ladders, then the clang of hatches being closed and doors dogged tight. Bessinger and I reached our gun at the same time, followed by Gibbon and the port gunner, and as usual Pappy was already at his station, tucking in his shirttails and cinching his belt. (Pappy never undresses at sea; he loosens his clothes and takes off his shoes, and that is the way he sleeps.) Gradually my eyes became accustomed to the darkness, and I could see the captain and Mr. Taylor on the flying bridge. Mr. Taylor was taking the reports of the stations as they called in manned and ready, and there seemed to be some delay on Gun Two, the 40-mm back aft.

"What's the matter?" I heard the captain ask. "Who's missing?"

Mr. Taylor relayed the question, then said, "Koster, sir."

"Send someone to find him," said the captain. "And report why he's delayed."

Mr. Taylor repeated this into the phone, then after a few moments said, "He's there now, Captain. Gun Two manned and ready."

"What kept him?" the captain asked.

Mr. Taylor asked the question, then said, "He couldn't find his galoshes."

There was a hiss like escaping steam as the captain let out his breath, then the intercom from the radar shack opened up.

"Range one oh double oh," the radar operator said. "Bearing zero six three."

So it was a radar contact. I'd assumed it was a sonar contact on the sub, but this was something else again.

"He's closing on us," said the captain. "He's headed right into the convoy."

The intercom opened up again, this time from the radio shack. "Voice message from the *Broome*," came the radio-man's voice. "He says show him your green, and tell him to turn east to avoid convoy."

"Acknowledge," said the captain, then through the speaking tube to the wheel house he said, "Come right to zero six zero. All ahead standard."

The ship shuddered as the engines increased speed, and with the radarman reading off the ranges and bearings we approached the contact. I couldn't help thinking of the *St. Augustine*, and I was glad to see the captain wasn't making a direct collision course. Finally the silhouette of a freighter loomed up out of the darkness, and the captain ordered the running lights turned on. Then, to Pappy, he said, "Give him an AA." This was the signal to identify himself, and Pappy sent it several times, but got no reply. By this time we must have been within two hundred yards of the freighter, and could see its outline clearly. Finally a wink of light appeared on its bridge, telling us to send our message.

"Tell him to steer due east to avoid convoy," the captain said, and Pappy blinked out the message. The man on the freighter acknowledged, and in a moment we saw the ship's outline begin to change, as it altered course. We watched for several moments, and then Pappy said, "Hey—isn't he coming toward us?"

He was right. Instead of turning east the freighter had turned due west, and was bearing down on us with what looked like the speed of an express train. The captain bent to the speaking tube and said, "All engines ahead flank!" and there was a jangling of bells and the ship leaped forward, but by now the freighter was towering over us and so close you could see the white of its bow wave. Nobody breathed for the next several seconds, then the freighter cut astern of us, missing us by what seemed like inches, and headed toward the convoy. "Get him on the light!" the captain shouted, but there was no answer on the freighter, and finally the captain turned to the 20-mm gunner behind him. "Fire a burst across his bow," he said.

"I can't," the man replied. "The gun ain't loaded."

"The gun—" The captain looked, and saw that Lincoln was still holding the magazine in his hands, as though posing for a picture. Before the captain could say anything there was a cackling in Mr. Taylor's headset, and he said, "Depth charges request permission to set on safe."

There was infinite weariness in the captain's voice as he said, "Permission granted." Then, to Pappy, he said, "Get the *Broome*, and tell them the ship disobeyed our orders."

"I think he knows that, sir," Pappy replied. "Look over yonder."

All through the convoy ships had turned on their emergency lights and searchlights, and we could see the freighter slowly making its way across the columns. Why there was no collision nobody knows, but after what seemed like a long time the stranger vanished into the darkness, leaving a shaken and disorganized group behind. The captain turned back to Mr. Taylor.

"I want you to give these men an hour a day drill in loading the 20-millimeter," he said. "By the time we reach New York, I want them to be able to have it uncovered, cocked, loaded, and ready to fire in seven seconds flat. Is that clear?"

"Yes, sir," said Mr. Taylor, quietly.

"Secure from General Quarters," the captain said, and then he added, "And I want Koster to make it from his bunk to his GQ station in fifteen seconds, regardless of what he's wearing."

"Yes, sir," Mr. Taylor said, again.

"All right. In the meantime, we just thank God that was a friendly, not an enemy." The captain had started to take off his binoculars when Linkovitch appeared on the bridge wing below.

"Sonar has a contact," Linkovitch announced. "Dead ahead, range eighteen hundred yards."

"So it's going to be one of *those* nights," the captain said, heading for the wheel house. "Sound General Quarters."

This time all stations were manned and ready in an instant, and those of us topside waited expectantly at our stations. The ship had slowed speed to one third; now it picked up again, and we could hear the orders being relayed to the depth-charge crew. We could also hear the ping and the echo from the sound stack, and the interval between them got shorter and shorter, producing a tension that grew like the tightening of a spring. Then there was no echo, meaning we were passing over the target; a bell rang back aft, and again, and two flaming explosions shot the K-gun charges out on either side. After a total of seven charges had been dropped the ship came around to the right, and the captain came out on the starboard bridge wing and looked back at our wake. Then the charges started to go off; the deck stung our feet as the shock waves hit the ship, and the whole ocean seemed to leap and slam about, sending up mountainous gray mushrooms of water. In the darkness it looked as though some writhing sea monster was following us, and I thought of our discussion of being in the water with charges going off. I was glad to be where I was, with several layers of steel between me and the water.

We circled back, trying to regain contact, but we might as well have been pinging in a bathtub. There was still the turbulence from our charges, and the roughening sea made it hard to keep the sonar beam steady, and all we could do was grope our way around, hoping to pick up a solid echo. But there was no luck, and the longer we searched the farther the convoy drew ahead of us.

Finally, we heard the intercom relay a message from the *Broome*, telling us to rejoin if we still had no contact, so we headed around, secured from General Quarters, and made the best speed we could to get back on station. There was a general feeling of letdown, because once having made a contact you want to stay with it, and our only consolation was that we'd kept the sub (or whatever it was) from doing any damage to the convoy. This, after our previous experience with the freighter, was at least a step in the right direction.

The rest of the night was routine, except that old Gibbon injured himself getting into his sack. It is the top one in a tier of three, with a leeboard on the side to keep him from being tossed out when the ship rolls; and he was just halfway over this leeboard when the ship slammed into a wave, giving him a jolt like being hit with a ball bat. He fell to the deck clutching himself, but everyone else just laughed, so after a few moments he picked himself up, tried to smile, and hobbled off to see Doc Newman. He reappeared later, proudly announcing he'd been bandaged. This time, he was extremely careful how he got into his sack.

Speaking of Gibbon, I found out the officers have their own name for him—they call him Old Zero. The word "zero," when he speaks it, is like something you can't describe; the "e" is stretched out into a kind of banshee wail, and when he has the wheel they always try to give him a course with as many zeros in it as possible, just to hear him repeat it. North, naturally, is perfect (000), but 040, 020, or any of those are almost as good, and it's reached the point now where everyone looks forward to his turn at the wheel. If he's aware of it he doesn't let on; he just sings out the courses as they're given to him, and remains as cheerful as ever.

Feb. 6—The big enemy in this part of the war is rust. You start off with your ship all sparkling and newly painted, and then up in the bow little spots appear, where the sea has rubbed the paint away. These turn to rust, which spreads, and as soon as you get a chance you chip away the old paint, wirebrush down to the bare metal, then put on yellow zinc chromate as a primer and gray over that. By the time you've got back aft the bow has started to rust again, and you go at it once more. You do it at sea if the weather permits; otherwise you do it in port, and if there is one sound more typical of a PC than any other it is the banging of the chipping hammers. Some PCs have more yellow on them than they do gray, and some look like spotted lizards, and the one thing you can be sure of is if you see one that's all gray it's either fresh from the builder's yard or is getting ready for inspection.

Feb. 7—We got a big load of mail today, but as far as I was concerned it was a bust. There was the usual letter from the family, saying how tough things were in the Island, and there was even one from Alice, saying how come I hadn't written, but the thing that really let me down was that Diane's letter was sort of run-of-the-mill as well. I don't know what I expected, but I'd come to look forward to her letters as something special, and this one was just sort of blah. Maybe it *has* been a tough winter, and I remember how sometimes in February and March you begin to get cabin fever and want to flap your arms and run in circles, but I'm here to state that from a distance that makes pretty dull reading. Diane ended her letter asking what became of the picture I was going to send her, so I looked up Doc Newman and asked him how he was doing with the roll. He kind of hemmed and hawed and cleared his throat, and finally had to admit he'd forgotten to take the lens cap off the camera, so the whole roll was one big blank. He was sorry, he said, but that's the way it was. I chewed on this for a while, trying to figure how to break it to her, but so far I've had no brilliant ideas. Doc said he'd try again some time, but at this rate the war will be over before he gets it done. It would be ironic if the entire course of my life was changed just because one man forgot to take the lens cap off his camera. I suppose stranger things have happened. I think I'm entering an introspective period.

Feb. 18—Off on another convoy. There's a kind of sameness about these things that makes it hard to write anything interesting, so I guess I'll just put down the unusual things if and when they happen. The Germans seem to have pulled most of their subs out of this area (most likely because of the convoys), so all we do is patrol back and forth on our station, *ping*—train—listen—*ping*—train —listen—talk about *dull*: you find yourself thinking of all sorts of things to do, just to keep your brain from turning to peanut butter. For example, I'm making an ash tray out of a cut-down 3-inch shell; I don't smoke, and I'm sure as hell not going to send it through the mail to anyone, but just the matter of polishing the brass gives me something to do, so here I am making an ash tray. And a couple of days ago I noticed the captain, on the bridge wing, scraping at a tiny speck of rust with his penknife. After a while Mr. Ferguson said to him, "Captain, you keep that up and pretty soon you're going to dig right through the metal. You been at it for two hours now."

The captain looked at him, smiled, and closed his knife.

"Wait till you get command," he said. "You'll find that until something goes wrong, you're the most useless man on the ship."

"I suppose you're right," said Mr. Ferguson.

"You know I am. You'll go out of your skull." He looked back at the spot and gave it a couple of extra scrubs, this time with his thumbnail.

Feb. 19—We saw a hospital ship last night, headed for Norfolk. It was all lighted up; you must have been able to see it twenty miles away, and as it crossed far ahead of us all I could think of was the guys on board, who were being brought back from the shooting war. The ship looked so sort of gay, with its white sides and bright lights and big red crosses, that it was hard to believe the people on board were in pain, or dying, or clobbered with drugs, but when you thought about it there was no other answer. It may have looked like a cruise ship, but it was sure as hell no cruise *I'd* want to be on. As I said before you can always think of someone who's worse off than you are, and I guess these guys were about at the bottom of the barrel as far as desirability was concerned. The only thing they could count in their favor was that they were going home.

March 3—A sort of embarrassing thing happened this morning. There's a Canadian corvette working with us, and when it got light enough to see through all the spray and drizzle we noticed he had his colors at half mast. Pappy was still in the sack, so Mr. Murray, the OOD, told me to blink across and find out who'd died. This was my first message under operating conditions, and I was careful to remember what Pappy had told me about not sending faster than you can receive. (If you try to show off and flip one out fast, you're likely to get a machine-gun-like reply, and it's mortifying to have to ask the other guy to slow down.) So I sent across a message that said simply, "Who died," and back came "The Secretary of your Navy." I relayed this to Mr. Murray, who told me to thank the corvette, and when I'd done that he told me to bring our own colors to half mast.

"Who was he?" I asked, loosening the halyards.

"Frank Knox," said Mr. Murray. "You'd think someone would have told us."

"You don't suppose they'll give us the week off, do you?" said Bessinger, who was on lookout.

"I wouldn't count on it," Mr. Murray replied.

Bessinger sighed. "Only asking," he said.

(On the subject of the Canadians, it's a real gas working with them. No matter how sloppy or terrible the convoy has been, they always send a message when we break up saying, "It's been a pleasure sailing with you," or something equally polite, and you even get the feeling they mean it. I'm told the British do the same thing, and even make little jokes every now and then. I guess anything helps.)

March 7—We got into New York last night, and the mail today was pretty thin. The only letter I got was from Miss Gresham, and at one point she said something that got me thinking so hard I didn't know how to answer. She was talking about all of us from the Island who'd gone in the Service, and she said, "You're all fighting for a noble cause, and the sacrifices you make now will be rewarded ten times over when Fascism is finally crushed." This didn't sound much like her, and I could only guess she'd been reading some sort of patriotic literature somewhere. But how to answer it was what stumped me. It's hard to think of yourself fighting for a noble cause when you're sitting in the darkness having icewater poured down your neck, but I suppose there must be something in what she said because otherwise so many people wouldn't have joined up. God knows I never liked what I'd heard about Hitler, but I'd never thought of this as a thing between him and me, and as for the guys in his submarines, whom we're supposed to be fighting, they're no more real than a problem on a blackboard. *Ping*—train—listen—target moving left—fifteen-degree lead angle—stand by to drop charges. . . . This whole thing is going to take some thought before I can give Miss Gresham any kind of sensible answer.

March 12—Old Zero really outdid himself today. He was on the foredeck, on rust-chipping detail, and had with him an electric wirebrush and also a bucket of yellow zinc chromate paint, with a line on the handle for letting it over the side. He plugged the wirebrush into an outlet, but he hadn't checked to make sure the switch was off, and the wirebrush started with a growl, caught the line on the paint-bucket handle, and turned the forward part of the ship into a whirling, yellow hell. Line, bucket, and paint swung around in a flashing, clattering arc, and by the time Gibbon, half blinded by the paint, had managed to grope his way to the outlet and pull the plug, the entire foredeck, the 3-inch gun, the ammunition lockers, the bridge wings, a part of the dock, and most of Gibbon were bright, dripping yellow. We all heard the noise and ran to see what happened, and by the time I got there Gibbon had his handkerchief out and was futilely trying to wipe the paint off an ammunition locker. He'd wiped his eyes clear, but the rest of his face glistened with paint, and occasional drops fell from the tip of his nose into the yellow paint on the deck. He looked like a large, sick canary.

March 17—Off to the south again. It's a cold, rainy day,

but the sea is calm and it's not bad below decks, so a lot of us gathered in the mess hall to pass the time. I brought out the letter from Miss Gresham and stared at it for a while, then turned to Pappy, who was writing a letter next to me. "Tell me something," I said. "What's this cause we're fighting for?"

He looked at me a moment before answering. "We got attacked," he said. "What else are we supposed to do?"

"My teacher says we're fighting for a noble cause," I said. "We're fighting to crush Fascism."

"I suppose you could put it that way," Pappy said. "When I was in the Pacific, we was fighting to save our asses."

"You ask me, I'm fighting so's I can get home," Bessinger said. "Just get the goddam thing over with, and go home."

Robbins, the Shipfitter, had been tuning his guitar, and he stopped long enough to say, "I don't go in for no fightin'; all I know is I get better chow here'n I ever had in my life."

"You look it, too," said Bessinger. "If we ever run outa charges, all we gotta do is drop you on the goddam sub and you'll split it wide open. Load you up on beans, and you're a one-man depth-charge attack."

Robbins grinned. "You're just sayin' that," he said.

"I'm serious," I said. "I got to answer this letter."

"Tell her we're fighting for Mom's apple pie and International Silver," Caulkins put in. "That's what the advertisements say."

"Say what I told you," Bessinger said. "Say there ain't one man here who wouldn't settle just for getting his ass back home."

"That would look kind of funny in a letter," I said. "She might misunderstand."

"Misunderstand what? It's the truth."

"O.K.," said Pappy. "Say it's the truth. There's still only one way we're going to do it, and that's by whipping the Germans and the Japs first."

Bessinger shrugged. "A detail," he said. "It ain't what we're fighting for."

Caulkins looked at him. "Suppose somebody said you could go home right now. Would you do it?"

"You bet I would," said Bessinger. "But who's gonna tell me?"

"I said suppose."

"Well, for one thing it's a long, wet walk from here to home," Bessinger said. "I'd have to wait till we got a little closer to land."

"You know what I mean."

"Sure I would. What good am I doing myself out here?"

"Even if you were the only one? If nobody else but you got to go?"

Bessinger considered this, then grinned. "Think of all the broads I'd have," he said.

"And you'd be the only guy in your block not in Service. That is, not counting the 4-Fs."

"So big deal."

"I still bet you wouldn't do it."

"It's a stupid question," said Bessinger. "It ain't ever gonna happen."

Napier, the Electrician's Mate who'd been a bartender, had been listening in silence, and now he said, "The way I look at it, a man's a lot safer out here than he is in the city. Out here the worst that can happen is you get sunk, but in the city you can be beaten, shot, robbed, run over, burned to death—"

"I know plenty of guys got burned to death at sea," Pappy put in. "Four cruisers full of 'em, off Savo Island. You could hear 'em for miles."

Napier stopped, and looked at him. "I didn't know about that," he said.

"I don't know where you been. *Quincy, Astoria, Vincennes, Canberra*—they called them the Sitting Duck Cruisers. I can still see it." After a moment he added, quietly, "And hear it."

"We're off the subject," Caulkins said. "We've got to help old Bowers, here, tell his teacher what we're fighting for. I vote for Mom's apple pie and International Silver."

I looked at the sheet of lined paper, at the top of which I'd written "Dear Miss Gresham," and suddenly the whole thing seemed impossible. "Forget it," I said. "I don't think she'd understand." So I wrote: "Thank you for your letter. It's nice to know you folks are behind us"—I stared at that for a while, then tore off the sheet and started again. The final letter, as I put it in the mailbox, read:

Dear Miss Gresham:
Thank you for your letter. I'm sorry I haven't been able to write more often, but things are kind of busy out here (ha! ha!) and we don't have too much time to write. But I do appreciate your thinking of me, and saying the encouraging things you do. Generally speaking I am well, and hope you are the same.

Your former student,
Ralph Bowers

March 29—Our time in Key West is usually pretty dull, but this trip was an exception. We'd no sooner moored at

Craig Docks than three men with sea bags came aboard; they were all Gunner's Mates First, and they were an answer to the letters we'd been wiring the Bureau ever since commissioning, asking for just one GM/1 to fill our complement. We didn't have room for all three, but the captain said they could spend the night and then two of them would have to go back to the barracks. The one we kept is named John Fox Humma, and he's part American Indian. I don't know the names of the other two, but you could just as well call them Some Disgusted. Lindquist, needless to say, is happy as a bug to have a senior GM to take over for him.

I had liberty next day, and decided it was now or never as far as getting a picture for Diane was concerned. If I didn't get one now she'd most likely lose interest, and that would be a stupid way to blow the ball game. So Caulkins, Gibbon, Linkovitch, and I set out in search of a photographer, after having had a couple of beers apiece to make sure we didn't get thirsty along the way. We finally found one of those photo parlors where they have all sorts of backgrounds, to make it look as though you were on board ship, running a locomotive, or whatever. We looked at the different choices, and finally Caulkins said, "For some reason I see you on a camel." To the photographer, he said, "I don't suppose you have a camel, do you?"

"No," the photographer replied, flatly. "No camels."

"Pity," said Caulkins. "Did you know that Key West is three hundred and twenty miles south of Cairo, Egypt?"

The photographer stared at him.

"I mean, in the circumstances, it would seem that a camel would be the *first* thing you'd have."

"I said no camels," said the photographer.

"How much do you charge for a picture?" I asked.

"One dollar," the photographer replied. "Or I'll do the four of you for three." I got the feeling he wanted to get rid of us as fast as he could.

"Hot damn," said Gibbon. "Ah'll send one to mah Uncle Roy."

"Why your uncle?" Linkovitch asked. "Don't you have a girl?"

"Sure ah got a girl. But she lives with Uncle Roy. The mail goes through him."

"Some romance," Linkovitch observed.

"Do you have anything that even *looks* like a camel?" Caulkins asked, and the photographer began to turn red. Two Shore Patrol, who'd been strolling down the street, stopped behind us.

"I tell you what," I said, quickly. "Let's all four get in this mockup boat, here, and pretend it's the 1208."

"Why pretend?" said Link. "Let's paint 1208 on the bow."

"You don't paint nothing," the photographer said. "You take it like it is, or get out."

"That's not very friendly," said Caulkins, then he, too, noticed the Shore Patrol. "Oh, very well," he said. "If you insist. Come on, lads, General Quarters."

With a certain amount of squeezing and laughing we managed to get into the boat, and the photographer took four pictures. We gave him three dollars, and as we walked away we inspected the results. In the first picture Gibbon had just noticed the Shore Patrol; he'd put both little fingers in the corners of his mouth and tugged his lips out like a rubber band, and in the other pictures he'd worked variations on the expression. Caulkins for the most part looked sick (he claimed he'd been trying to look like a camel), while Linkovitch and I seemed to have eaten something sour. We shuffled the pictures about, trying to decide who got which.

"Look at it this way," Caulkins said, to me. "It isn't so much what you send her, it's the fact you went to the trouble to have it taken. I think you ought to get the first one."

"Thanks," I said.

I'm still trying to phrase the letter to go with it.

Then yesterday morning, just as we were ready to shove off on the northbound convoy, it turned out that Mr. Campbell was missing. He'd gone ashore the night before, and Mr. Taylor said he'd made some remark about having "found something" on the beach, but that was all anyone knew. The captain looked at his watch, and estimated the time to the rendezvous point, then set Special Sea Details and ordered the lines singled up. We waited, with the engines turning over, and finally the captain gave the order to take in the lines. Slowly the ship began to move away from the dock, then someone shouted, "Here he comes!" and down the pier, running at what looked like forty miles an hour, came Mr. Campbell.

The ship was perhaps six feet away from the dock; if it kept going Mr. Campbell would miss it and automatically be up for a General Court Martial, whereas if we stopped now he might be able to make it. After a second's hesitation the captain ordered the engines stopped; Mr. Campbell sailed out over a widening eight feet of open water, and landed spread-eagled across the after lifelines. When he regained his breath he reported to the flying bridge, where, very quietly, the captain told him he'd be restricted to the ship in New York. He said, "Yes, sir," and went below. I'd say that three-quarters of the crew wished we'd kept on going.

March 31—The captain has developed a new pastime to lighten the boredom: he shoots at flying fish. In southern waters we're always running into schools of them; they explode around our bow and skitter away in all directions, gliding over the wave tops and every now and then flicking their tails in the water for an added push. The little ones look like so many butterflies, and they go as far as the first ripple before they go smack on their noses and vanish, but the larger ones can glide for quite some distance and at a good speed, and they make a target that is just about impossible to hit. Yesterday the captain brought a .30-06 Springfield rifle onto the flying bridge, loaded a clip into it, then sat and waited. In a few minutes a dozen or so flying fish sprayed away from our bow, and the captain had just time to flick off the safety, take aim, and squeeze off one shot before they were gone. Needless to say he missed, but not by a great deal. The next time he managed to get off two shots, one of which hit the water just ahead of a fish and soaked it with the splash, and then he looked around and saw Mr. Campbell behind him, holding a Thompson submachine gun.

"O.K. if I have a try with this?" Mr. Campbell asked.

"Be my guest," the captain replied. "The next covey's yours." He seemed to be amused at something but I didn't realize what until later.

Mr. Campbell waited, the Thompson gun cocked and at the ready, and when the next group of fish hit the air he started firing. He fired a long burst, which drove the muzzle of the gun upward and destroyed his aim, but what was puzzling was at first there were no splashes in the water. Then, after what seemed like a long time, they appeared, a flutter of spray that was nowhere near where the fish had been. He looked at the gun and then at the captain, who was grinning broadly.

"That gun's got no muzzle velocity," the captain said. "You'd do better to throw baseballs at them."

"Then what the hell good is it?" Mr. Campbell asked.

"It's for close-in fighting. The low velocity will knock a man down, but you can't aim it worth a damn."

Mr. Campbell made a sound of disgust, then handed the gun to Humma, the new Gunner's Mate, who was standing by. "Clean it," he said, and went below.

(On the subject of flying fish, they're supposed to make good eating although kind of bony. I've heard that on some ships they leave a lighted flashlight on deck at night—something you could never do in a convoy—and then in the morning pick up the flying fish that've been attracted by the light. It makes, if nothing else, a different kind of breakfast.)

We later saw some dolphins, but naturally didn't shoot at them. One was a mother with a baby; she spotted us from far off and came toward us with long leaps, while Junior tried his best to keep up. You could almost hear him crying "Hey, Ma! Wait for me!" but she didn't slow up; she came straight at us and zoomed into our bow wave, and after a while Junior caught up with her and joined the fun. It took him a while to get the knack, but soon he was as good as she. Gibbon, who was on the sound stack, claimed he could understand what they were saying to each other. For some reason, I don't entirely disbelieve him. The only bad thing you can say about dolphins is that they'll frighten the bejeezis out of you at night, because when they come at the ship their phosphorescent wake makes them look like a torpedo. Many a lookout has literally wet his pants at the sight of the luminous streak heading for the ship, and before he can even shriek "Torpedo!" it's changed course, and is playing in the bow wave.

April 5—Well, I sent the picture off to Diane. I told her about the Doc's foulup with his lens cap, and the trouble we went through getting the picture in Key West (although I couldn't mention the name of the port), but nothing I could tell her did anything to change the expression on my face, which looked as though I'd just sucked a lemon. And Gibbon, of course, gave the whole picture an air of insanity that made us all look drunk. It was a ticklish letter to write, and I only hope I got away with it. That's one of those things that time alone will tell.

April 10—There's been a whole slue of promotions, some of which are for the good and some of which aren't. I made Signalman Third, so now I have a nice fat crow to wear on my right sleeve, but at the same time Pappy made Chief, which means he'll have to be transferred because we don't rate a Chief Signalman on a ship this size. He'll probably go to a DE, which is good for him, but it'll leave me leading Signalman on board, with only a couple of halfass strikers to fill out the watch list. The idea of *me* being leading Signalman is enough to make you burst out laughing (or crying, I'm not sure which), but if I have to do it I guess I can.

The captain made Lieutenant Commander, which means *he's* got to leave, so Mr. Ferguson will take command and Mr. Taylor will be exec, and a new Ensign will come to round out the roster of officers. This is either good or bad, depending on what the new Ensign is like, but it's kind of ominous because it puts Mr. Campbell next in line for executive officer, and that would be a complete disaster.

Ferguson this seemed to hold true. We had two stragglers in the first hour; one had an engine casualty and had to be escorted back to Ambrose Channel, and when we finally rounded up the other one it turned out he needed a doctor. He sent us a message saying, "What do you do with a man with 105° fever?" and while we were relaying that to the Coast Guard cutter *Icarus*, which carried a doctor, the merchant ship sent: "What do you do with a corpse?" From the *Icarus* we got: "Suggest burial at sea if refrigeration is impractical," and as far as we know that was the end of the matter, except that the ship continued to lag behind.

Then, during the midwatch the first night, Mr. Murray had the deck, and he suddenly said, "Call the captain—the convoy's gone crazy!" It appeared that, while we were holding a straight course, the convoy was circling around us, and although this didn't make sense the readings from the gyrocompass confirmed it. The captain appeared from the wardroom, checked the gyro, then compared it with the magnetic compass, which being non-mechanical was reasonably accurate. Then the reason was clear: the gyro, for the apparent hell of it, had started spinning out of control. The captain called Napier, the Electrician's Mate, who shut off the gyro and set about repairing it, and we settled down to using the magnetic. It had its drawbacks but it was better than nothing, and it was certainly better than looping all over the ocean the way we'd been doing with the gyro. That kind of stuff can lead to collisions, and, as the old saying goes, a collision at sea can spoil your whole day.

Three days later, the sonar crapped out. Nobody knew what caused it; it just quit pinging, which left us about as useful to the convoy as one of those swan boats in the Boston Public Garden. The only advantage came more or less by mistake—the *Icarus*, ahead of us, dropped charges on what had looked like a sub but was actually a school of red snapper, and the surface of the water was thick with dead fish. Since we were no good to the convoy we stopped and picked up as many fish as we could; guys were hanging over the side with potato sacks, orange crates, boathooks, swab handles, lassos—anything, in fact, that would pick up a fish. They weren't all red snapper; there were some of those rainbow-colored tropical fish, and there was a small hammerhead shark, but the snapper was the main delicacy, and we finally got enough so that each man had his own fish for supper. Caproni got in the spirit of the thing and started to cook them all different ways, but after about the fiftieth fish he just rolled them in flour and fried them, and any man who wanted it done a special way had to do it himself. There was only one casualty: Gibbon had tied two fishing poles together, and while reaching as far outboard as he could he lost his balance, and toppled into the water. By now, things like that are so routine with him that it passed almost unnoticed; he swam to the stern and climbed up on a screw guard, and from there someone gave him a hand onto the deck, and that was that. He continued fishing as though nothing had happened.

The day before we got into Key West Mr. Murray and Mr. Campbell had a fight that almost turned into a slugfest. Their dislike of each other has grown since the day they met, with Mr. Campbell considering Mr. Murray a Momma's boy (which in a way he is) and Mr. Murray considering Mr. Campbell a lecher and an operator (which in a way *he* is), and each one considering the other a disgrace to Yale (Yale men, it turns out, have no sense of humor about their college). At any rate, it's a rule of the ship that the officer on watch has to wear a shirt, and Mr. Campbell, who'd been sunbathing on the signal bridge, came to relieve Mr. Murray without putting his shirt on. He just said, "O.K., Sonny, I'll take over," which aside from everything else is sloppy procedure.

"You can't relieve me till you've put your shirt on," Mr. Murray told him.

"Oh, come off it," said Mr. Campbell. "What's base course?"

"Put your shirt on, and I'll tell you," said Mr. Murray.

"Oh, Murray," said Mr. Campbell with infinite weariness, "why don't you take my shirt and blow it out your ass?"

"I'll tell the captain!" Mr. Murray shrieked, and the two of them went pounding down to the wardroom, leaving nobody in charge of the deck. The lookouts continued to scan their sectors; I tried to think what I'd do if a sub should suddenly appear ahead of us, and all the time we could hear the two officers shouting at each other down in the wardroom. Then there was quiet, and in a few moments Mr. Murray returned, his face as red as a ripe tomato, and resumed his post by the speaking tube. We didn't see Mr. Campbell the rest of the day, and it was clear the captain had chewed both their asses out right up to the third rib.

June 6—We were just south of Hatteras this morning, with a smoky horizon and a long, oily sea, when the squawk box opened up from the radio shack, and an excited voice said, "Hey, it just came over—we invaded Europe!" The word went around the ship in a matter of seconds, and someone turned on the commercial radio and piped it into the p.a. system so we could all hear, but there was very little beyond that one fact, and the recording of General Eisenhower's announcement. I got to thinking about the guys in the infantry, and the guys in the amphibs who

94

took them ashore, and I felt almost ashamed to be sitting here—fat, dumb and happy, and in no more danger than if I were crossing Main Street back home. (You'll notice I said "almost" ashamed; I'm not so stupid I want to be a dead hero.) Then the captain realized that Mr. Taylor, who'd had the midwatch, was still in his sack and had missed the news, so he sent Linkovitch below to tell him. Link came back in about two minutes, trying to keep a straight face.

"Did you tell him?" the captain asked.

"Yessir," Link replied, making a note in the deck log.

"What did he say?"

"He said, 'I kind of figured we'd do that.'"

"That's all?"

"Yessir. He went back to sleep."

The captain started to say something more, then gave a small shrug, opened his penknife, and began to scrape at a rust spot on the bridge wing.

We listened to the radio all the rest of the way, but about all we could make out was that the landings were successful and that so far our guys were holding their own. (Speaking of the commercial radio, there's a station in the Carolinas somewhere that has this fruity announcer who drives everybody bughouse. He's on the morning show, and whenever he gives the time he says, "It's seven fifteen—or whatever —don't be late for school and don't be late for work, and keep your CHIN up out there!" The last thing you want to hear, when you're either hoarse from puking or soaked to the bone with icewater, is some breezy bastard telling you to keep your chin up. I suppose he means well, though. Thinks he's contributing to the war effort.)

June 9—It now turns out that the invasion forces had a really hairy time on one beach, and for a while it looked as though they might not make it. When we got to New York we saw the newspapers, which were naturally full of pictures, and while the action shots were mostly blurry I saw one that gave me plenty to think about. It showed a PC right in close to the beach, and that wiped out the idea I'd had that PCs were used only on slow convoys. Apparently they're also used in invasions, to set up a line of departure from which the barges can head for the beach, and in conditions like that you might as well be in the infantry. That's one thing about being in the armed forces: the minute you think you've got it made, someone sneaks up and snaps the rug out from under you. It's the finest kind of living, if you don't mind ugly surprises. At least we're still this side of the Atlantic, so we don't have too much to worry about for the next week or so (ha! ha!).

June 12—The ship is going in for overhaul, and the captain is giving as many men leave as possible. I'm in the first batch to go, and I must say I can hardly wait. After what seems like years of living cooped up in a compartment with a lot of other guys, hanging on so you don't get thrown out of your sack when the ship rolls, getting up at all hours of the night and being soaking wet most of the time—to say nothing of every now and then being scared out of your drawers—the idea of sleeping in your own bed, having home-cooked food, and being able to hack around whenever you want is almost too good to be true. And girls—imagine seeing real, live, clean girls! I've heard a lot of theories about girls in the last little while, and I think maybe now's the time to put some of them to a test. I mean, after all, what can I lose?

One more thought: I can take all these diary pages home with me, since they're now beginning to clutter up my locker, and give them to Miss Gresham to keep until the war's over. That way she can go over them and perhaps do a little correcting, in case I should some day want to print them. And in case I don't come back . . . well, we won't think about that.

June 23—I'm not sure the idea of having leave is a good one. It's great to look forward to, and I suppose it is good to break up the ship's routine, but life at home is so completely different that it takes a while to adjust. At home you're another person from the one you used to be; your outlook is different, and things that used to be fun seem kind of pointless. Then, when you get back to the ship, the things you do *there* seem stupid, and you do them automatically and only because you've been taught to. The really frightening thing is how easily you fall into the military routine once you're back, and in almost no time it's as though you'd never been home. The whole thing is unsettling, to say the very least.

My leave was an anticlimax almost before it got started. The Navy's setting up a practice bombing area on the Island, so I was able to hitch a ride on a Navy plane and save that long day on the train, bus, and boat. I'd phoned the folks I was coming, but since I didn't know my E.T.A. (estimated time of arrival) I had to call them again from the field. They arrived in about fifteen minutes, Mom all dressed up like she was going to church, and Dad looking glum because he'd just discovered the spare tire was flat, and it was so old it wouldn't take any more patches. There was a lot of small talk after Mom finished weeping, and all the way into town she told me the various things that had happened since I'd left, none of them particularly world-shaking. Dad asked a few questions which only showed how little he knew about the Navy, and then he began to brood about where he might get another spare tire.

Everything at home looked the same yet somehow different, and every time I sat down I got up again, as though the chairs were on fire. Mom was fussing around, trying to do things to make me comfortable, and I finally decided it would be easier on all concerned if I went out and took a little walk downstreet, on the pretext of getting some air. I changed into civilian clothes, which were too tight, and went out, figuring there'd be some action at the Spa.

The first person I ran into was Alice, coming out of the drugstore, and for a second she didn't seem to recognize me. Then her eyes went wide and she said, "Well, look who's here! I thought you were in the Navy."

"I am," I replied. "I got a week's leave."

"Well, fancy that." She moved off, and I put out a hand to stop her.

"What are you doing tonight?" I asked.

"Tonight I'm busy." She started away again.

"What about tomorrow?"

She hesitated. "Call me tomorrow, and we'll see."

Under any other circumstances I'd have told her to go stuff it, but as it was I figured I had to make every day count, so I said, "O.K. Tomorrow it is, then."

She went off, and I drifted over to the Spa, which was full of Coast Guard, guys from the Navy bombing range, and over-draft-age Islanders. The phone booth was full, so I slid over to the bar. Nobody even looked at me, and it took a while before George, the bartender, came my way. He wiped the bar in front of me and said, "What'll it be, Ralph—a Coke?"

"Gimme a Bud," I said, as casually as I could.

"How long you been twenty-one?" George asked. "Last time I heard, you was sixteen."

"That's a long time ago. I'm an old man now."

"Show me an I.D. card says you're twenty-one and I'll believe you; otherwise don't bother me. I'm busy."

"God damn it, the Navy doesn't worry about that kind of chickenshit!" I shouted. "Do I have to put on my uniform before you serve me?"

"You have to put on about four-five years," George replied. "This ain't the Navy, and I ain't serving you."

One of the Navy guys looked at me. He was an Aviation Gunner's Mate, and he had a face like a mashed potato. "What's the matter, mate?" he said. "He giving you a bad time?"

"You heard him," I replied. "He thinks a Signalman Third's too young to have a beer."

The Gunner's Mate looked at George. "Gimme a Bud," he said. "And a glass."

"I can't serve that kid," George replied. "He ain't of age."

"I'm not asking you to serve him. Gimme a Bud, and be quick about it or I might get impatient."

George opened a bottle and slid it across the bar, a glass upended on its neck. "It's my license, you know," he said. "I'm the one whose ass is out if he's caught."

"You get your T.S. card at the Chaplain's office," the Gunner's Mate said, and handed the beer to me. I thanked him and offered to pay him, but he waved me aside. "Next time wear your uniform," he said. "It impresses the draft dodgers."

"Listen, you," said George, turning red. "I don't have to—"

"You bore me," the Gunner's Mate said, and turned away.

The phone booth was empty by this time, and I took my beer and called Diane's house. After several rings a voice said, "Hello?" and I realized I wouldn't recognize Diane's voice unless she identified herself.

"Diane?" I said.

"No, this is Effie. Diane's over to Harry's. I guess."

"Oh."

"Who's this?" I sensed it was a younger girl, probably her sister.

"This is Ralph Bowers," I said. "Just tell her I—"

"Ralph Bowers?" There was a shriek of laughter. "You mean the one with the goony friends?"

"I don't know," I replied. "What—I mean—"

"The one who sent the picture?"

"Oh, that. Yes, I guess so."

Another shriek of laughter. "I'll tell her," said Effie; then there was a click and the line went dead.

Diane called next morning, and for some reason I knew who it was the minute I heard her voice. "Welcome home," she said, and after I'd mumbled something she went on, "I got your picture."

"So I gather," I said. "Your sister seemed to think it was pretty funny."

"It doesn't take much to make Effie laugh." I didn't quite know how to take this, so I waited and she went on, "How long are you home for?"

"A week," I replied. "What are you doing tonight?"

"Tonight I'm busy. How about tomorrow?"

"Finest kind. I'll pick you up after supper."

With that settled, I decided to straighten out a few things with Alice. Alice and I had at one time been going more or less steady—that is, I usually took her to the movies, and we'd done a certain amount of wrestling around in the sand dunes at Dionis—but the way she'd acted yesterday made it clear she'd either lost interest, or was trying some weird sort of come-on to make me jealous. In either case it didn't really matter, but I was curious, and as I've said I wanted to make every minute count while I was on leave. I had a feeling there'd be plenty of times I'd kick myself for *not* having done something I could have, so there was no point passing up possibilities on some minor technicality. I called her, and got the same distant voice she'd used before.

"What are you doing tonight?" I asked.

"I take it Diane is busy," she replied.

"What's that supposed to mean?" I knew perfectly well, but I wanted her to say it.

"Just what it says. You wouldn't be calling me if Diane was free, would you?"

"What makes you think that?" (It happened to be the truth, but I saw no point dwelling on it.)

"You sent her your picture, didn't you?"

"Oh, for God's sakes." That picture had apparently done more mileage than any since Pearl Harbor. "I sent it because she asked me to. And there were three other guys in it, since it's so important."

"You don't have to tell me. I know all about it."

"All right. She asked me for a picture, and I sent her one. Did *you* ever ask me for a picture?" There was a short silence and I knew I'd scored a point so I went on, "And what's more she wrote me three letters for every one you wrote, so I think the least she deserved was a picture. Do you have any objections?"

"None in the least."

"Then what's all this snotty tone about?"

There I tore it. It's one thing to score a point over a girl and it's another thing to rub it in, and by taking it one step too far I blew the whole ball game. "As far as I'm concerned you can step straight to hell!" she shouted, and I could almost hear the crash as she slammed down the phone.

I got out my bike and my surf rod and rode out to Surfside, but the tide was wrong and the fish weren't biting, and after casting for about an hour I got a bird's-nest in my line the size of a pumpkin, so I said the hell with it and came home. I spent the rest of the afternoon trying to unsnarl the line, and finally had to cut it. After supper I put on my uniform and went down to the Spa, where a new guy was tending bar, and I got swapping sea stories with one of the Coast Guards. By the time the evening was over he was my best friend, so I guess I must have been a little smashed. Usually, we refer to the Coast Guard as the Hooligan Navy.

The next night I managed, by all but going down on my knees, to get Dad to let me take the car. I had to promise not to take it off the hard-top roads, not to go over 45, not to have anything to drink (there'd been a big stink about my beer breath last night), and to be back by midnight—he'd originally said 10:30—and all these I agreed to in order to have something to take Diane out in. I mean, it's all right to walk a girl around if you've been dating for a while, but for the first time it's an absolute necessity to have a car, and while it isn't a *guarantee* of success only a fool would try anything without it.

I didn't have to be told that my big problem lay with Harry Coffin, and while it irritated me to have to compete with a lousy civilian (what was he, anyway—4-F?) I decided not to harp on the subject, but instead assume he had some good reason for not being in the service. Just take it easy, I told myself, and don't force anything.

The Dreamland Theatre ("All Talking, All Singing, All Dancing") was showing a Fred Astaire picture called "The Sky's the Limit," and I thought that might be as good a way as any to start the evening. Diane was prettier than I'd remembered, and there was something about her eyes that made her seem to be always on the verge of laughing, and as we took our popcorn and settled into our seats I felt that this might be the beginning of Something Big. Then the lights went down, and for a while you couldn't hear the picture because of the thunder of kids running around in the balcony and up and down the stairs, but finally things settled down and we were able to hear what was going on. Once or twice I slid a hand in Diane's direction, but the first time I got her popcorn bag and the second time I got snarled in the folds of her dress, so I gave up and decided to save the physical contact until later. I decided the slow and easy approach was probably best in the circumstances.

When the picture was over I asked if she'd like to drive around a little, and she said sure. There was low-lying fog but you could see stars overhead, and it occurred to me that if we went up to Altar Rock we could probably get a pretty good view. As we cut off into the moors from the Polpis Road I cleared my throat and then, as though it had just occurred to me, I said, "What's Harry doing these days?" I said it as though I was concerned for poor old Harry, who had some deformity that kept him out of uniform.

"Harry's in the Marines," she replied.

Bang. End of that approach. "I thought he was still around," I said. "Your sister told me—"

"He was. He had a week's leave before shipping out."

"Oh." I digested this information. "Where's he going?"

She shrugged. "Where do they all go? The Pacific, I guess."

"We may be going there, too," I said. I didn't believe it for a minute, but I also didn't want to be so to speak left behind.

She looked at me with interest and said, "You mean that little boat of yours? Could that go all the way to the Pacific?"

"I should hope to tell you. And it's not a boat—it's a ship."

"What would you do?"

"This and that. PCs are used for a number of things. Invasions . . ." I left it there, as though I'd already said too much. "We're an all-purpose ship," I concluded. "We have to be ready for anything."

She laughed. "The picture certainly made it look that way. If ever I've seen a motley crew, that was it. Did you ever think of showing it to the Germans?"

"What do you mean?"

"It'd make them die laughing. If they thought that's what they're fighting against they might let down their guard, and then you could go pop-pop-pop, and wipe 'em all out."

I saw nothing particularly funny in this but I couldn't think of a reply that didn't sound stuffy, so I concentrated on my driving. The rutted road snaked across the moors and finally rose above the fog, and ahead of us we could see the low hill that's called Altar Rock. The sky overhead was bright with stars, and the fog looked like a ghostly lake lying in the hollows on the moors. I thought of the times I'd looked at those stars at sea, and it all seemed to have happened to another person in another country in another century. My thoughts were brought back to earth by the rattling of loose stones as we made the final approach to Altar Rock, and then there was a bang and a hiss and the car felt suddenly heavy. We made it to the top of the hill, and I set the brake and got out, but I didn't need to look to know that the left rear tire had gone flat. I reached in for the ignition keys to open the trunk, and saw Diane looking at me in the darkness. I couldn't believe she was about to laugh but that's what her eyes looked like, and for a moment I wondered if perhaps changing the tire might wait.

"Yes?" I said. "You were going to say something?"

She shook her head, still with that odd air of amusement. "Nothing important," she said. "It can wait."

"This won't take a minute. Can you give me the flash from the glove compartment? I've got to—" The sentence died in my throat, as I remembered Dad's grousing about the spare tire being flat. "Oh, no," I said, quietly. "Oh, no. Oh, Judas Priest."

"What's the matter?" Diane had the flashlight poised in mid air, and I snatched it from her and fumbled to get the trunk open. I shone the light on the tire, which looked like a badly stuffed snake, then hit it with my fist. It was soft as a pillow. Slowly, I closed the trunk.

"We have two choices," I said, when I'd explained the situation. "We can walk from here to the main road and hope for a lift, or we can drive until the tire comes off the rim, and then walk. You name it."

"I don't mind walking," she replied. "It seems kind of silly to destroy a tire. Let's just leave the car here."

So we took the keys and left the car, and walked down into the fog and southwest toward the 'Sconset road. Under other circumstances this might have developed into something interesting (there's a spongy growth called mattress grass in the area, and it forms a thick ground cover on which you can do all sorts of interesting experiments), but as it was all I could do was try to think of ways to get that tire repaired before Dad missed the car. Nothing I thought of was any good, because he was up before the boys reported for work at Gordon's garage, and he wouldn't buy any story about my having run out of gas. Then I wondered if the Coast Guard or Navy might have someone who could help, but since this wasn't Government business I didn't see any duty officer springing a man loose. I was faced with the simple fact that my ass was in a bucket of live steam, and all I could do was try to lessen the pain. I finally delivered Diane to her house and then went home, feeling like a man about to be executed.

Everyone was asleep when I got in, but it seemed as though I'd no sooner gone to sleep than it was daylight, and Dad was shaking me and asking about the car. "I'll tell you about it later," I said, trying to buy a little time. "Everything's all right."

"You'll tell me about it now," he replied. "What happened?"

So I sat up, scrubbed my hands over my face, and went through the whole story. When I was finished, there was a short silence.

"You went off the hard-top road," he said, at last. "That was something you promised not to do."

"I know," I replied, "but it was foggy." It wasn't good but it was quick, and it made him think a moment.

"What's that got to do with it?" he asked.

"We had to get out of the fog, and Altar Rock was the only place."

"I don't see what that has to do with it."

"Did you ever try to talk to someone in the fog?" My father is a rational man, and anything completely irrational tends to throw him off balance. He scowled.

"How much did you have to drink?" he asked.

"Nothing. We went to the movies, then went to Altar Rock to get out of the fog. It's as simple as that."

He pondered this, then said, "As far as I can see, you're crazy. The Navy must have done something to scramble your brains." He left the room shaking his head, and I went back to sleep. Everything considered I came off better than I'd expected, but needless to say I didn't get the car again.

The rest of my leave consisted of inconclusive talks with Diane, a certain amount of hanging around the Spa, and finally a visit to Miss Gresham, to whom I delivered my diary pages and from whom I got a pep talk on the meaning of democracy. I didn't see Alice again, which was all right with me.

It seems a strange thing to say, but I was almost glad when the week was up and I reported back to the ship. At least on the ship you know to a certain extent what to expect, and after one day of being back it didn't seem as though I'd ever been away.

The first night, some of us who'd had leave gathered back on the fantail to chew the fat and exchange experiences. We'd first gone to the mess hall but it was too hot, so we took our coffees and our Cokes topside, and sat around the depth charges. Robbins brought his guitar, and plucked at it in a half-hearted way while the others talked. Someone asked him what he'd done on leave and he just grinned and said, "Nothin'," and for a while there was just idle conversation, as though each man was sorting out his memories and trying to decide which to tell. Then Bessinger launched forth on a lurid description of an encounter he'd had with three girls in Brooklyn, and from then on everyone thought only of how to top him.

"A funny thing happened to me," said Lindquist, when Bessinger paused for breath. "I was on the—"

"It better be funnier than last time," Napier cut in. "You just got over that dose you picked up in Miami."

"I was on the Staten Island ferry," Lindquist continued, ignoring the interruption, "when this old guy came up and asked if I knew the way to Cleveland. I told him—"

"Is Cleveland still in the first division?" Linkovitch asked suddenly. "Last I heard, they was five and-a-half games behind."

"They're way down," Humma told him. "Headed for the cellar."

"At any rate—" said Lindquist, and Link said, "Son of a bitch. There goes my bet."

"So I told this guy—" Lindquist raised his voice slightly.

"Who cares about Cleveland?" said Napier. "Didn't you meet any broads?"

"Let me *finish*," Lindquist said.

"Ah met a funny kind of broad," Gibbon put in. "At the bus station in Apalachicola, she had this little old dog on a leash—one of them dogs about the size of a grapefruit— and ah tripped over the leash and went right on mah kisser. Well, sir, she picked me up and dusted me off, and before ah knew it ah was in the—"

"Don't tell me you were in the sack," said Bessinger. "I'll believe anything, but not that."

"No, ah was in the jug," Gibbon replied. "She started hollering ah'd molested her, and the SPs come an' carted me off. Missed mah bus, and had to wait a whole day for another one."

"The hell with it," said Lindquist, to nobody in particular.

"You know what I heard," Caulkins announced. "I heard we're going to be transferred."

"Who's we?" said Humma. "I just got here."

"The whole ship," Caulkins replied. "We're going to another area."

There was a brief silence, then Bessinger said, "Where?"

"I don't know. But this morning I heard the captain and Mr. Taylor talking, and the captain said, 'All I know is they say it'll be hot.' Then Mr. Taylor said, 'I better get out the charts,' and he went into the wheel house."

"Charts won't do him much good till he knows where we're going," Linkovitch observed. "There's lots of places where it's hot."

In a sort of sleepy voice, Robbins spoke up. "I wonder if he means the weather is hot, or the action is hot," he said. "That could make a big difference."

There was another silence, then Bessinger said, "God, I hope it's not the Pacific." The hottest fighting right now is in Europe, but nobody's forgotten that the Pacific is still crawling with Japanese.

"I suppose we'll know pretty soon," said Caulkins. "If they change our address from Fleet Post Office New York to F.P.O. San Francisco, then we'll know it's the Pacific."

Napier started a long story about a woman who'd once come into his bar wearing only a slicker and tennis shoes, but everybody's mind was busy and pretty soon the story petered out. He turned to me, and said, "We haven't heard from you, Bowers. Did you knock 'em cold back home?"

"Oh, sure," I replied. "Nothing but dames everywhere I turned. Had to beat 'em off with a stick."

He laughed. "That's the good thing about living in a

small town. Just put on your uniform and you're a conquering hero. If you live in the city, it's another story."

"I guess it must be," I said, and let it go at that.

July 8—It's confirmed we're going to another area, and while there's nothing official the best guess seems to be Panama. Our address is still F.P.O. New York, and Mr. Taylor had Linkovitch checking the charts of the Caribbean with special emphasis on the Canal Zone, so that would seem to be the way to bet. Koster, the Radioman with the scar on his shin, has put in for a transfer on the grounds of chronic seasickness, and the captain said he'd approve it if he could get a qualified replacement. That shouldn't be too hard, because Koster was not what you'd call an addition to the ship's company. He did his job, but just barely.

I've started a training program for Leemy and Slater, my two Signalman strikers, and I've found that half the battle lies in giving them confidence in themselves. They're still so new they're frightened of big waves, and they don't yet know how to duck so that the worst of the water goes over them. They just stand there, clutching at anything, and get drenched, and Leemy in particular gives me the feeling he's about to burst into tears. Signals and flag hoists they can learn; how to behave at sea is still way beyond them.

Ensign Potter, the new Communications Officer, turns out to have a kind of pixie sense of humor. When you encode a message you have to put what's called padding at the beginning and the end, so that anyone trying to break the code won't have anything sensible to start with, and Mr. Potter likes to put things in his padding to needle the Regular Navy. In one recent message, for instance, his opening padding was "Annapolis laddies," and the closing one was "Slap my wrist," and the captain looked at the message a long time before he initialed it. "I'm probably a fool to do this," he said as he finally scribbled his approval. "But somehow I can't resist. You'll either go a long way in the Navy, Mr. Potter, or you'll be a Seaman Second by August."

"I have nothing to lose," Mr. Potter replied. "It's your signature."

"That's what I mean by going a long way," the captain said, and handed him the message.

July 15—We're off, to Panama by way of Key West and Guantanamo. The fighting in Europe has made the Germans pull most of their subs out of this area (one, just south of Hatteras, sends out periodic weather reports and that's all), and the convoy business is zip. Two other PCs and we formed what was technically known as Convoy NK 633, but there were no ships for us to escort so we ran three abreast at standard speed, and everybody lay on deck and worked on their suntans. At one point, off Norfolk, a big 2100-ton destroyer appeared out of the haze, circled us once, then opened up with his light. I took the message, which was: "Rank curiosity—what are you doing?" I told the captain, who had me send back: "Believe it or not we are Convoy NK 633 three escorts no ships," with which the destroyer replied: "Where are your carriers?" The captain had me send: "Gone for the mail," after which the destroyer cut ahead of us and pretended to act as our escort until he disappeared. Some war.

Speaking of mail, I got a letter from Diane before we left New York, in which she said how nice it had been to see me and how sorry she was about the various foulups. It wasn't as funny as some of her letters but it wasn't a bad one either, and it made me think that perhaps everything wasn't lost. At any rate it'll be worth keeping up the correspondence. Needless to say, I heard nothing from Alice.

July 23—We left the other PCs in Key West and, after refueling and taking on water, we set off alone for Guantanamo. We made the quick, overnight trip from Key West to Cuba, then ran down the east coast so close we could smell the jungles, rounded the southeast tip of the island, and turned westward to the entrance to Guantanamo Bay. There's a gate ship there, guarding the antisubmarine nets, and you have to wait for permission to go either in or out. The signals were against us when we arrived, so the captain called down for the engines to stop. The engine-room telegraph bells rang but the engines kept going, and the captain repeated the order with no better effect, so he put the ship in a wide turn and sent someone to look for Mr. Campbell. Finally, just about as Mr. Campbell arrived on the bridge, the engines stopped, and the captain was white with rage.

"Who's on duty on the throttles?" he asked.

"I'll see, sir," Mr. Campbell said, and disappeared. He came back later with some elaborate story about how one of the snipes had had to go for coffee, and another was mopping up some oil spill and couldn't reach the throttle, and the captain simply stared at him during the whole recital. Then, when he had finished, the captain took a deep breath.

"Listen to me carefully," he said. "Listen to every word. If that ever happens again, every man on duty in the engine room—and you—I repeat and you—will be court-martialled. Is that clear?"

"Yes, sir," said Mr. Campbell, turning red.

"And I want to see you in my cabin after we've docked."

"Yes, sir."

"That's all."

Mr. Campbell left the bridge. I later saw him trying to chew out one of the snipes, but the man barely listened to him. As Pin-Head pointed out so long ago, when you play buddy-buddy with the men you lose your ability to discipline them. Mr. Campbell might as well have been a Fireman Second for all the respect he commanded. (And, on the subject of Pin-Head, Mr. Campbell didn't recommend him for promotion because of some argument they'd had. Pin-Head swears he's going to get him near the rail some night, and push him over the side.)

August 2—From Guantanamo to Panama is a trip of about eight hundred miles. You go due south between Jamaica and Haiti, then southwest across the Caribbean until you spot the Panama sea buoy, which is no mean job at night because it looks about the size of a candle. Then you pick up the green range lights which line you up with the entrance to the Canal, and run in on them until you're in the harbor. Our berth is at the Sub Base in Coco Solo, and from there you have to take a bus into town to make liberty. You go to Cristobal, which is in the Canal Zone and under U.S. authority; the rest of the town is called Colon, and belongs to the Republic of Panama. About the only difference is that the juicier night spots are in Colon, while the bus stop is in Cristobal, right next to the pro station. That way, nobody can claim he forgot to take a prophylaxis; the station is staring at you when you go for the bus. It's not romantic, but it's better than a dose. (For what it may be worth, Cristobal Colon is Spanish for Christopher Columbus. Big deal. He never even landed here.)

August 15—Our duty consists of escorting the Panama–Guantanamo convoys, which is about as exciting as the final days of the New York–Key West run. There hasn't been a submarine around here in a year, so all we do is shepherd these ships along and try to keep them from running into each other. We also try to keep them clear of bigger ships, going at high speed for the Canal; usually we succeed, but sometimes it gets a little hairy. The big ships come so fast they're on you before you can get a light message to them, and we had one tanker that came crashing through our convoy like a whale through a school of scup. Why he didn't hit anyone, nobody knows. Leemy was on signals at the time, and I thought he was going to faint.

August 23—I got a letter from Miss Gresham today, saying she thought there were real possibilities in my diaries. She said there were some places where I'd tried too hard to be a writer, and others where I hadn't tried hard enough, and come to think of it I guess she has a point. In the future I'll have to remember to try not to be too arty, and at the same time not to be sloppy. It's a neat balance, if you can work it. I always thought you just wrote, and there it was.

August 27—Mr. Campbell has taken to wearing his .45 automatic when he's on watch. (Every officer has a .45, but they usually wear them only at GQ.) The captain asked him what this was all about, and Mr. Campbell muttered something about cleaning the gun when he came off duty. I don't know who slipped him the word, but it's clear he knows someone's out to get him.

This last trip to Guantanamo, by the way, was a bone-crusher. We had only one ship to escort, a high-speed transport, and when he asked if we could make 15 knots the captain said of course. The only trouble was we were going directly into a northeast chop, with a brisk wind and seas about as resilient as concrete, and the entire trip was one continual pound-pound-pound. The 3-inch gun, forward, was driven upright by the sea, which also wrenched the ready ammunition locker loose from the deck and slammed it against the pilot house, and an SC who was with us lost his mast and had to turn back. (The SC, being 110 feet and made of wood, felt this kind of kicking around worse than we did.) About 95% of our crew was seasick, and at one point I made my way back to the mess hall and was greeted by a total shambles. Benches, plates, pitchers, clothes, and cutlery were strewn around as though by a giant eggbeater, and under the table in one corner, smeared with the debris of a plate of peanut-butter-and-mayonnaise sandwiches he'd been trying to make, was Caproni, holding his head and moaning, "Oh, dear God in Heaven, why didn't I join the Marines?" There was nothing I could do, so I clawed my way forward and climbed into my plunging sack. The compartment smelled of wet clothes, sweat, and puke, but if you buried your head under your pillow you shut out the worst of it. Sleep, of course, was impossible, because you had to keep hanging on so's not to be pitched out onto the deck. It was something like living inside a washing machine.

September 6—Today being my eighteenth birthday, I've become eligible for the Draft. I don't suppose it makes much difference, but I'm told you have to have a Draft Registration card no matter if you're in the service or not, so I went and asked Mr. Taylor what I did about it. He looked blank, and said, "God, I don't know. Why don't you forget it?"

"I can't," I replied. "There's a penalty for not registering."

He thought for a moment, then said, "I'll find out," and vanished. I've a feeling I'm going to have to keep after him.

The rainy season is about on us. Once a day, late in the afternoon, the skies open up as though someone had turned on a fire hose; it rains for maybe twenty minutes and then the sun comes out again, and all the roads and puddles give off steam. As the season progresses the rain starts earlier and lasts longer, until finally everything is just a sea of rain and red mud. Then—or so they tell me—the whole thing stops, and you don't see rain again for another year. But while you see it, man, you see it.

Sept. 10—I saw Mr. Taylor again today, and he knew before I spoke what I'd come about. "There's no place you can register here," he said. "As far as I can tell, you'd have to go over to the Pacific side." He said it as though I'd have to go to the Aleutians.

"Then may I have a pass, sir?" I said. "I'd really like to get it done."

He looked at me for a long moment, then shook his head and started to write out a pass. "If it were anyone else I'd say it was an elaborate excuse to get drunk," he said. "With you, I'm afraid it's got to be real."

"Yes, sir," I said.

He handed me the pass. "Good luck."

Sept. 11—What a day. The train to Panama City and Balboa looks like something out of an old Western movie, and the first thing that confused me was the presence everywhere of the signs "Silver" and "Gold." In the waiting room, over the drinking fountains, by the toilets, always one saying "Silver" and another "Gold," and I didn't think too much about it until I used a drinking fountain marked "Silver." Then a guard came up and began to give me a hard time in Spanish, and I finally, from an American petty officer, found out what it's all about. It seems that when the Canal was being dug there were laborers from all over the world—China, the Caribbean, Africa, South America, the United States, wherever—and the colored laborers liked to be paid in silver coins because they took up more space and made a louder jangle in the pocket. The whites were perfectly happy to be paid in gold, one small coin of which was worth a whole mess of silver, so when segregation set in those words were used instead of Colored and White. (There'd been no segregation at all in Panama until the United States arrived; in one Panamanian family there might be all shades from ebony to snow white. But then there'd been no Panama, either; that country was created by a U.S.-inspired revolution—courtesy of T. Roosevelt—which split it off from Colombia and made it into a country we could deal with about the Canal.)

All in all it was an informative train ride, and the petty officer left me with the impression I hadn't even started to learn anything. The one thing he couldn't tell me, which I asked him when we parted, was where I went to register for the Draft. He looked at me as though I was crazy, and muttered something about District Headquarters and then took off.

District Headquarters was in Balboa, in the Canal Zone. I asked the duty Yeoman, and he looked up Selective Service in the phone book, then directed me to what turned out to be a small office over a store that sold Panama hats. There was an American flag on the wall, and a framed picture of President Roosevelt, but the man on duty was obviously Panamanian, and just as obviously puzzled at my being there.

"I want to register for the Draft," I said.

"You live here?" he asked, pronouncing "live" like "leave," and giving me the wrong impression of what he was saying.

"No, I'm not leaving," I replied. "I only got here a little while ago. But I just turned eighteen."

He stared at me. "You turn eighteen what?"

"Eighteen years old. I have to register for the Draft."

"So how come you wear sailor suit?"

"I'm in the Navy. But I need a Draft card."

He closed his eyes, and shook his head as though to clear it. "Where you come from?" he said, at last.

"My home is in Nantucket." I might as well have said I lived in a tree.

"You go home. They give you Draft card there." This, for him, ended the conversation.

"I just *was* home, but I wasn't eighteen," I said. "There's a penalty if I don't have a card."

"Go home," he said, closing his eyes again. "Go home, go home, go home."

"I can't! I'm on a ship in Coco Solo!"

He put his fingers in his ears, and shook his head violently. "Go home!" he repeated, over and over.

There was a long pause, during which neither of us moved.

"Well, nobody can say I didn't try," I said, finally, and went downstairs. I looked in the window of the Panama hat store and wondered if Dad would like one, then thought what he'd look like with a hat like that in Nantucket, and dropped the idea.

It turns out that several good beers are made in Panama, and each company has its own beer garden. I got into a place called the Balboa Gardens, and before I knew it it was time to start thinking about the train. I went out, just in time to get caught in the afternoon downpour, and by the time I finally got aboard the train I was wet both inside and out. I slept most of the way across, and arrived on board ship looking like a survivor of a first-class marine disaster. Mr. Taylor was at the gangway when I came aboard, and he looked at me with an appraising eye.

"What luck?" he asked.

"Not too much," I replied, and went below to change.

Sept. 15—There was a weird, almost spooky meeting in the mess hall tonight. Rinaldi, the Chief Motor Mach, has made Warrant Officer, which means he'll be transferred any minute now. He'd been celebrating at the Chiefs' club, and had bought the usual cigars for the ship's company, and then he and the snipes and some of the other guys had gone down to the mess hall. I joined them a little later, and I could hear all conversation stop as my feet touched the ladder. Then they saw who it was, and after a moment Pin-Head turned to Rinaldi.

"You're the only one can do it," he said, in a low voice. "You're one of them now, and you can talk to 'em like an equal."

"Like hell I can," Rinaldi replied. "You know better'n that."

"Still, you can tell them," Pin-Head insisted. "*Somebody's* got to tell them."

"I'd do it, but I haven't been aboard long enough," Humma put in. "It ought to be someone with more time."

"What's this about?" I asked, and all eyes in the room turned toward me. I felt as though I was in a smoky den of wolves. There was a short silence.

"What happens when the captain's transferred?" Pin-Head asked, quietly.

"I didn't know he was going to be," I replied. "Where's he going?"

"He hasn't been—yet. But these ships change captains about every six months."

119

"So?" I said.

"So who makes captain?"

"Mr. Taylor."

"And who makes exec?"

"I'd thought of that," I said. "Mr. Campbell."

"That's right. How would you like that?"

"Not much."

There was another silence. Pin-Head ground out the butt of his cigar on a plate, then said, "There's some of us wouldn't take it. We'd ask for transfers, we'd go over the hill—we'd do anything. If that son of a bitch was to make exec, we might even mutiny."

"No, you wouldn't," said Rinaldi.

"You don't think so?" Pin-Head glared at him. "Don't make any bets."

"Ah don't think ah'd mutiny," Gibbon said, from a far corner. "Ah'd just cut mah throat."

"We think the Chief ought to tell Mr. Taylor," Pin-Head went on. "None of us can do it, but with his new rank he can say things he couldn't before."

Rinaldi belched, then sighed. "Well, I'll take a stab at it," he said. "But not tonight. This is gonna require some thought."

"Give it all the thought you want," said Pin-Head. "Just do it, is all we ask."

Sept. 19—It's funny how a message can get around a ship without anyone saying a word. All today people have been cheerful, and while nobody's said anything specific, it's clear that something good has happened. The first tip-off I had was when I heard Pin-Head singing after breakfast, which is a time he usually reserves for coughing and spitting and generally unpleasant noises. I asked him what was up, and he looked at me out of the corner of his eye, sang, "Oh, what a beautiful mornin'," and waltzed away. Guys were laughing more than usual, Mr. Murray seemed to be purring like a cat, and there was a certain amount of horsing around, and I finally decided that if Pin-Head wouldn't tell me then maybe Caulkins would. I found him at his desk, which is across from the Radioman's. Koster's replacement, a Radioman Second named Altschuhl, was sorting through the message files.

"What's the good word, Cork?" I asked.

Caulkins glanced at Altschuhl, then said, "Nothing special. Why?"

"The whole ship's acting like the war was over, or something."

"Maybe it is. Nobody tells me much."

"Like hell. What's it all about, or can I guess?"

"Your guess is as good as mine."

I was about to say something more when a figure appeared in the doorway, and I looked around and saw it was Mr. Campbell. He was wearing his .45, and he looked paler than usual. His suntan, on which he worked so hard, seemed to have faded away.

"Caulkins, do you have my file there?" he asked.

"Yes, sir," Caulkins replied. He opened a filing cabinet drawer, and under P-16 (Personnel) found a folder with Mr. Campbell's name. He gave it to him, and Mr. Campbell riffled through it, then handed it back.

"Have you written any letters about me recently?" he asked.

"About you? No, sir."

"Or in any way having to do with me?"

"No, sir."

Mr. Campbell paused, thought for a few moments, then turned and left.

"What was *that* about?" I asked, after he was out of hearing.

Caulkins shrugged. "Search me."

It was a while before I found out the story. It seems that Rinaldi had told Mr. Taylor how the crew felt, and Mr. Taylor had thanked him and said nothing more. Then Mr. Murray, whose hatred of Mr. Campbell was such that he simply couldn't keep quiet, let slip the fact that Mr. Campbell's transfer was already in the works. Apparently there's an officer at the PC assignment desk in the Pentagon who can accomplish shortcuts, and avoid a lot of involved paper work that a PC isn't prepared to handle. Normally if an officer is unsatisfactory he must stand a General Court Martial if there are serious charges against him, or be given an unsatisfactory fitness report at the next reporting period, and this leads to charges and counter-charges and a lot of unpleasantness all around. A PC is too small for such a major headache if it can be avoided, and the officer on the assignment desk—an old PC hand himself—knows how to cut corners and ease the anguish. Our captain called him on the telephone (apparently some time ago, when Mr. Campbell first started wearing his .45) and explained he had this officer who, although he did some things well, had a personality problem that made it impossible for him to become exec. The PC assignment man told the captain how to write the necessary letter, which the captain did one night on Caulkins' typewriter, and that was that. It's now just a matter of waiting for Mr. Campbell's orders, and his replacement. They could replace him with Hitler, and it would still be an improvement.

Sept. 28—Green and Lincoln, our two Steward's Mates, almost got in deep trouble last night. They were in La Florida, one of the two big Blue Moon joints in town (the other being the Copacabana), and somehow a fight developed that came close to having international results. First I should explain about the Blue Moon joints: they're sort of night clubs, with a cruddy show every now and then and dancing the rest of the time. There's also a big bar, and this is where a good deal of the business goes on. The "hostesses," who double as chorus girls, will dance with you in exchange for dance tickets, or if you prefer to sit at the bar they come up to you and say, "You buy me dreenk, honey?" and if you agree they order what's called a Blue Moon. This comes in a brandy glass and is mostly Coca-Cola, for which the bartender charges you a buck. In theory, if you buy enough Blue Moons or enough dance tickets she'll take you back to her place after closing, but I've never heard of that working out. The usual routine is she tells the poor sucker to wait while she changes her clothes, then she skins out the back door and leaves him standing there, ten or twenty or thirty bucks poorer than when he came in. Of course it's mostly officers who get this shafting, partly because only they can afford it and partly because there's a 10 p.m. curfew for enlisted men, which wipes us out for any late work. For enlisted men, those in a hurry, and other riffraff there's a short, dimly lighted street, lined on both sides with cribs that look like horse stalls, where the girls look out the top halves of the doors when they're not busy. I once saw a picture of hell by a Dutchman named Bosch, and it had much the same feeling.

At any rate, Gibbon and Caulkins and Linkovitch and I were passing La Florida when we heard sounds of a ruckus going on inside, and we slowed down to see what was happening. After a moment the swinging doors banged open and a figure came spinning through, crashed to the sidewalk, then leaped up and ran back, pulling a knife.

"Hey!" said Caulkins. "You know who that is—it's the bouncer! Somebody bounced the bouncer!"

"He's gonna wish he didn't," Gibbon observed. "Ah think there's gonna be a lot of blood around shortly."

There was more noise inside, and some girls screamed, and Linkovitch moved closer to the door. "I can't see a damn thing," he said.

"Better stand back," Gibbon told him, edging away. "This is the kind of situation where ah seem to wind up gettin' hurt."

"Still, it's gotta be worth seeing," Link replied, standing on tiptoe. "This kind of thing don't happen too often."

The doors flew open again and Lincoln, the junior Steward's Mate, staggered out, holding a hand over one eye. Then came Green, walking slowly backward while he fought off the bouncer and the bartender, both of whom had knives. They were crowding at him through the narrow doorway, and when they got outside they spread out to surround him. In a flash like a panther Green grabbed each man by his knife wrist and gave them a monstrous snap; the two men screamed and flipped over onto their backs, and lay moaning on the sidewalk. Green looked at them, dusted off his hands, then saw us.

"Hi there, mates," he said. "Where you been all evening?" He looked at the people crowding in the door of La Florida, then said, "I think we'll be going now." In the distance, a police whistle shrilled. He took Lincoln by the arm and started off, and when we moved to join them he said, "You guys better let us go on alone. We're kinda hot property right now." He led Lincoln down an alley, and they vanished into the darkness.

"Let's go back and see what they did to the joint," Link

said. "I bet that Green just naturally took it apart."

"Ah got a better idea," Gibbon replied. "Let's not. That place is gonna be crawlin' with police right soon, and for some reason they always kinda home in on me. Ah think ah'll just stroll along and take the air."

There were SPs at the bus station when we started back for the Base, and they were watching everybody who got aboard. Any colored man they'd take out of line and question, and there was a civilian with them who apparently came from La Florida, because he'd shake his head when they were brought to him to identify. We didn't see Lincoln or Green, and we wondered how they could possibly avoid being caught. It was getting near curfew time, and unless they showed up soon they'd have the added problem of being absent over leave. We thought about them all the way back to the Base, wishing we'd been able to do something to help.

When we reached the ship we went down to the mess hall and there they were, Green standing by like a mother hen while Doc Newman held an ice bag to Lincoln's swollen left eye. "Hey!" said Linkovitch. "How'd you make it? They got the whole Panamanian army out looking for you."

"We grabbed us a ride on a Navy truck," Green replied. "We got back before the word was out."

"What happened?" Link asked. "It looked like you had a small war on your hands."

"Green saved my life, that's what happened," Lincoln replied, from under the ice bag. "If it wasn't for him I'd be dead."

"Don't be a silly horse's ass," Green said. "I didn't save nobody's life."

"You sure as hell saved mine," Lincoln said. "And don't try to tell me no different."

"What *happened?*" Link repeated.

"Some honky civilian didn't like us in there," Green said, in a matter-of-fact tone. "But he took a bad way to show it—he hit old Lincoln, here, in the eye. So I flattened him." He shrugged. "That's all."

"Like hell it is," said Lincoln. "Tell about the knives."

"He pulled a knife," said Green. "So I had to break his arm."

"And the bartender, and the bouncer—" Lincoln's voice began to rise.

"Who' tellin' this story, anyway?" Green asked, irritated.

"You are, but you ain't tellin' it all. You saved my life."

"If I'd known you was gonna carry on like this, I'da left you there. Now, shut up and let the Doc fix you." Green turned away and poured himself some coffee, and drank it with a noise like a horse at a trough. It was only then I noticed that his hands were trembling.

"Hot damn," said Lincoln, with a small laugh. "You shoulda seen them guys flyin' through the air. It was just like the circus."

"I'll say one thing for goin' out with you," Green said, pouring himself more coffee. "It don't take much to amuse you."

Oct. 5—We had a queer thing happen on the way up to Gitmo (short for Guantanamo). I still don't know how to figure it out, and I guess nobody else does either. It was at night, about halfway between Panama and Jamaica, and the sea was calm and the visibility good. All of a sudden, way off to port, a small, white flare rose above the horizon, hung for a second, then dropped back. Bessinger, the port lookout, reported it, and Mr. Potter, who had the deck, got a bearing on it and then called the captain. In a minute another flare appeared, and then a third, all on the same bearing, and after notifying the convoy commodore the captain changed course and brought the ship up to full speed, to go and investigate. The closest land was Nicaragua, about five hundred miles away, so these flares had to come from a ship of some sort, or perhaps a lifeboat, or—and this was a long chance but a possible one—they could have been fired by a sub, hoping to lure us into range where he could knock us off. Subs had done that before, so it wasn't out of the question. Whatever it was, it was technically a distress signal, and not to be ignored.

The minute the ship changed speed everyone knew something was up, and dark shapes began to appear on deck. One minute the foredeck was empty, and the next there were four men standing around the 3-inch gun, looking out ahead. The captain had the word passed that we'd come to GQ in twenty minutes, so very quietly the gun covers were removed, the ammunition made ready, and pretty soon the whole topside complement were gathered near their GQ stations, quietly waiting. The captain figured the flares had to be fifteen or twenty miles away, so there was no need for an immediate GQ. The radar and the sonar searched both sides of the bow, looking for a contact either above or below the surface of the water.

When, finally, GQ was sounded, the hatches were dogged shut and the blowers turned off, and a quiet settled in that was broken only by the hammering of the engines and the racing of water past the ship's side. Neither radar nor sonar had any contact, so after a while the captain said to stand by to fire star shells. The first one was fired to port; there was the blinding flash (from which we hid our eyes) and the blast of hot air and the ringing of the deck plates, and then, high in the sky, the shell exploded in a burst of dazzling blue-white light that parachuted slowly to the surface of the water, illuminating everything beneath it. Those with binoculars searched but could see nothing, so a second shell was fired, this time dead ahead. Then a third, to starboard, but the results were the same: nothing visually, nothing on sonar, and nothing on radar. Whoever had fired the earlier flares had simply vanished. We cruised around the area for a while, then rejoined the convoy. If it was a real distress signal, we were too late; if it was a trap, we were lucky. We'll never know which.

Oct. 15—Mr. Campbell's orders and his replacement were waiting for us when we got back from Gitmo. His replacement is an Ensign named Donath, who looks something like a young Abe Lincoln and gives the impression of knowing more than most Ensigns. (I can remember the time when I was impressed by an Ensign just because he was an officer; I now know that a lot of Ensigns couldn't find their ass with both hands, and are saved only by the Chiefs or senior petty officers in their divisions.)

Apparently the whole thing was no surprise to Mr. Campbell; either the captain told him in advance or he got wind of it through the scuttlebutt, because when his orders were delivered he showed no more emotion than if they were just another piece of mail. Caulkins had to type up the endorsement detaching him from the ship, and he said there were none of the fireworks some of us had been expecting. The captain signed the endorsement, and handed the orders to Mr. Campbell; they shook hands, and the captain wished him luck, and he left. He was subdued but not sullen; he said goodbye to a couple of the snipes and went ashore, saying he'd send someone around for his gear later on. Most of the crew just stared at him as he left, and Pin-Head and Mr. Murray were among those who were nowhere to be seen. Rinaldi had already been detached, so he missed the whole thing. For the first time, I felt slightly sorry for Mr. Campbell; he knew that most everyone was gloating over his departure, but he tried to carry it off like he was just leaving for the weekend.

Caulkins said the orders sent him back to the Submarine Chaser Training Center, in Miami, for reassignment to the Amphibious Pool in Little Creek, Va. The Amphibs are, naturally, the bottom of the barrel as far as desirability is concerned; they're the ones who run up on the beaches during invasions.

Oct. 30—The war in Europe must be pretty nearly over, because more and more ships are coming through the Canal on their way to the Pacific. As they approach the Canal they carry on various kinds of war games, the idea being to see if they can sneak up without alerting the Army, who are in charge of the area defense. Once or twice, on convoy, we've had flares dropped on us by a patrol plane that mistook us for an incoming task unit, and all I can say is it's lucky we don't have any trigger-happy gunners. We're so far from any real war that you've got to think three times before you shoot at anything, but there are some guys who'll start shooting at the sound of a cap pistol, and not really care what they're shooting at. One theory is it's fear makes them do it, and I wouldn't be surprised. Once fear gets started, it's like a brush fire.

Speaking of the real war, our guys started back into the Philippines ten days ago, making landings on the island of Leyte. Then a good part of last week there was a naval battle going, in which the Japs took a real kicking around, so it looks like that part of the war may be heating up just as the European part winds down. There's talk that the Japs have started using some sort of suicide tactics, diving their planes into our ships, but nobody could be that crazy for long, so I don't imagine it'll amount to anything. All I'm sure of is I'm glad we're not there.

Dec. 17—There has been flat zero to report until today. Even the mail has been nothing unusual—the folks report that Dad finally got a used spare tire for the car; Diane reports the autumn colors were brighter than last year (what became of those funny letters she used to write?), and Miss Gresham reports that the Fascist beast is being driven back into his lair. For someone who harps about writing direct, precise sentences, she sure as hell can get overblown when she wants to. I wonder if teachers ever go back and re-read their own writing.

At any rate, today is Sunday, three years and ten days after the Japanese attack on Pearl Harbor, and at 0715 we're awakened by the sounds of aircraft zooming low over the harbor. We run topside, and the sky is full of planes from one of our carriers—gull-winged F4Us, and fat-bellied TBM torpedo planes—making a mock attack that's an exact duplicate of the one three years ago. They buzz the Canal locks, they practically tear the tops off the trees, and they make strafing runs on every military installation in sight. There are nothing but Navy planes, and nowhere is one single Army plane to be seen. Not one. (We found out tonight that one Army P-38 did get off the ground, ran out of gas, and had to make a forced landing.) The attack lasts for maybe twenty minutes that seems like an hour, and then the Navy guys go looping back to their carrier, most likely laughing themselves silly. From the way they *fly* they seem to be laughing; they're all over the sky like a lot of drunken butterflies. (One came so close to us that, when he zoomed straight up after his pass, I could see the pilot and his yellow Mae West lifejacket.) If the Army is as bone-deep stupid as this would make them out, we're in for a long and gritty war. The cheerleaders at Nantucket High could have done a better job of defense.

Dec. 20—I may have spoken too soon about the European war winding down. The Germans seem to have caught the Army flat-footed up somewhere in Belgium, and have knocked a great big hole in their line and are headed for the Channel. Maybe we transferred the Army guys who were in charge of the Canal defense and put them in Belgium, because it looks like the same kind of foggy thinking they showed here. Find a chance to screw something up, and the Army will do it for you every time. (I don't mean to imply the Navy is perfect in this respect, but at least when you're at sea you have time to think of an excuse before the rest of the world finds out.)

Mr. Donath, the new engineer officer, has been looking at Robbins, the Shipfitter, in an odd way ever since he first saw him. They both come from the South, but Mr. Donath is from Virginia and Robbins is from Kentucky, and there doesn't seem to be much in their backgrounds that would have brought them together. Still, Mr. Donath keeps looking at him like he'd seen him somewhere before, and this afternoon he came out with it and asked the question.

"No, *sir*," Robbins replied, scratching one bare foot with his guitar. "I don't recall us having met." As an afterthought, he added, "Leastwise, not when I was sober."

"Were you ever in Roanoke?"

"You mean Roanoke, Virginia? No, sir. Not that I can recall." Robbins thought a moment, then said, "Less'n I come *through* there on my way to boot camp. I come through a lot of strange cities on that train."

Mr. Donath shook his head, started away, then said, "Do you have a brother?"

"No, sir. But I have a sister, if that'd help."

Mr. Donath laughed, and walked off. Robbins watched him go, his eyes not leaving Mr. Donath's back.

"What was all that about?" asked Bessinger, who'd overheard the conversation.

Robbins shrugged. "He's a mite confused," he said, and began to pluck on his guitar.

Dec. 25—This was a kind of glum Christmas. The weather was bright and hot but nobody felt very festive, and the presents we'd gotten through the mail looked out of place when we opened them. I don't know why, but they looked kind of pathetic. They were dog-eared reminders of home, which is so far away it seems like something imagined in a dream, and the only good thing I can say about the day is at least there weren't any of those miserable red Christmas-tree lights we saw in Miami last year. The Panamanians take a more religious approach to Christmas, and while the effect is somewhat different it is still shabby. Nothing looks worse than tinsel in bright afternoon sunlight, but if you put a gun at my head I couldn't tell you why.

Added to the generally sour taste of the day was the grim fact that the Germans seem to have broken our lines wide open, and are crashing around in Belgium pretty much like they owned it. If they get to the Channel it could be Dunkirk all over again, with the British and us being chased into the water, and after that only God knows what. I heard the captain and Mr. Taylor talking, and the captain said he'd heard someone at the Officers' Club say it looked like the Germans had managed to come up with an atomic bomb, because nothing else could have smashed our lines so completely. I don't know what this atomic bomb is, and if I asked the captain I'd have to admit I'd been eavesdropping, but I gather it's something so powerful it'll take the place of a number of regular bombs. The Big Brains on both sides have been trying to put one together, and it now looks like the Germans have won. If you ask me, it's another example of our Army's stupidity—if we'd wanted an atomic bomb, we should have gone to the boys at some good college, like Harvard or M.I.T., told them what we had in mind, and then, when they'd made it, let the Army in on the secret, with full instructions on how to use it. That would cut the foulup chances to a minimum (if the instructions were in big print), but to let the Army in at the very beginning is just handing the whole thing over to the Germans. The more you see of the way we can screw things up, the more you wonder if we've even got a chance of winning this war. Someone once said that wars aren't won; they're lost by the side making the most mistakes, and if that's true we've got that end of it sewed up cold.

There was a halfway hopeful note on the radio tonight, saying that we've stopped the Germans at a place called Bastogne, but that's something that could change by tomorrow morning. I remember the radio in the early days of the war, saying that the British or French were "retiring in good order to previously prepared positions," or "straightening their lines," and "making minor tactical adjustments," all of which were simply sweet talk for the fact they were getting their asses kicked from here to breakfast. The guys who write the radio news can find any number of syrupy ways to paint a bright picture of disaster.

January 6, 1945—(The slogan for this year is "Home Alive in Forty-five.") We had an unusual thing happen on this last convoy: we ran over a palm tree. It was a clear night, with the sea so calm you could see the stars reflected on the surface, and there was a following wind that blew the exhaust smoke ahead of us. Suddenly, with no warning, there was a bump and a crash and a bang, and then the ship began to vibrate. The officers came squirting up on deck like peas out of a pod, some going forward and some aft, asking anybody who might have seen what happened. Finally, after talking with the lookouts, Mr. Murray (who had the deck), Leemy (the signal watch), and the guys on the ready gun aft, as well as checking in the lazarette for screw noises, the captain pieced together the whole picture: There'd been this floating palm tree (in the rainy season a lot of trees get washed into the sea, and the circular current keeps them moving around), and the only parts of it above water were a few branches and the roots, all of which were hidden by our exhaust smoke. We ran over the trunk, hitting it at right angles, and it tore out the sonar head like a rotten tooth, then folded over the starboard propeller blades like a spaniel's ears, leaving a lot of palm matting wound around the shaft. But we could still use the port engine, so we turned on our breakdown lights, eased away from the head of the convoy, and told everyone we'd see them in Panama much later.

As far as the captain was concerned, the most embarrassing thing was the radio report he had to send to Coco Solo, telling them he'd hit a palm tree in the middle of the Caribbean and would be a little late getting home. Even Mr. Potter knew better than to put any of his anti-Annapolis padding in that one.

So now we're in drydock, having a new sonar head installed, our shafts checked and propellers replaced, and getting a new coat of plastic anti-fouling bottom paint. About all you can say for it is it's a change.

Jan. 30—Someone knows something we don't know.

The yard crew finished the repairs, then instead of going back to our berth we were sent to a work dock, where they started making alterations. They removed the two forward K-guns and replaced them with 20-millimeters; they installed a five-mile-range loudspeaker on the flying bridge; they put in a complicated p.a. system between the flying bridge, wheel house, radio room, radar shack, sound stack, wardroom, and crew's mess hall; they painted the hull a darker gray; and on the bow they painted over our numbers, which had been about two feet high, and replaced them with monster figures over three times that size. It all points to one thing: we're headed for the Pacific, because none of those changes has anything to do with duty in the Atlantic or Caribbean.

My own reaction is to say all right—we've had a year of easy duty, so now it's only fair we try something else for a change. Besides, the Pacific isn't *all* bad; I understand there are PCs doing mail runs down around the Solomons, and there are all sorts of things to be done that don't necessarily lead to trouble. It's a big ocean, and we've got a lot of ships there, and only so many of them can be in trouble at one time. And anyway, after what happened at Leyte Gulf, the Japanese may not have too many ships left by the time we get there. I've been in the Navy long enough to know it's stupid to think too far in advance; things can change so fast there's no point making plans, so the best thing to do is eat whenever you get the chance, and leave the worrying to others.

Linkovitch's reaction is a little different. He figures he owes the Japs a good poke in the snoot for the time he spent in the lazarette of the capsized *Oklahoma*, and he hopes we get some kind of duty that'll give us a chance to shoot at them. Lincoln, on the other hand, is terrified.

Green took the news without emotion. He hasn't made liberty here since he and Lincoln got in that dust-up at La Florida, and as far as he's concerned Panama has less than nothing to offer. For him, the Pacific can't be any worse. I think that, taken as a whole, the crew have become so bored with this duty that they look forward to anything that'll bring a change. Gibbon, in fact, is unashamedly excited. "Hot damn," he said, when the scuttlebutt reached him. "It looks lak ah'll win mah bet."

"What bet?" said Caulkins, who'd been the one to tell him.

"With mah uncle. He was in the Navy in what he calls the Great War, and we got a bet to see which of us gets furthest away from home."

"How far'd he get?" Caulkins asked.

"Portsmouth, New Hampshire."

Caulkins stared at him. "You sure you don't have that bet won already?"

"Ah ain't paced it off, but this'll sure as hell put it on ice. He be fit to piss green."

Caulkins tried to think of something to say, but could only nod in silent agreement.

Leemy and Slater, the two Signalman strikers, came to me to see if the news was true. "It looks that way," I replied. "And so what?" I figured that, with them, I'd better act extra casual. "Signals are the same in the Pacific as anywhere else."

"Yeah, but it's a bigger ocean," said Slater.

"What's that got to do with it?"

"I don't know." Slater looked at Leemy, who said, "We just wondered."

I was sorry I wasn't chewing tobacco, because this would have been the time to send a stream of juice over the side.

Instead I just spat, but the wind was wrong and the effect wasn't very good. "Look, fellows," I said, wiping my chin. "You got nothing to worry about. I'll back you up any time you need help, and if the Old Man tries to chew you out just tell him to come to me—I'm responsible for you, and I'm the one who'll answer." It was a brave speech, meaning absolutely nothing.

"That's all very well," Slater said, "but what about the Japs?"

"What about them? By the time we get out there, there may not *be* any Japs. We're not going into battle tomorrow, you know. We'll be a long time getting there, and you never know what may happen in the meantime."

"Yeah," said Leemy. "You never do."

I looked at them the way I imagined a Marine drill sergeant would look at a couple of recruits. "What the hell's the matter with you guys, anyway?" I snarled. "You chicken, or something?"

"No, *sir*," Slater said, quickly. "We were just wondering."

"Well, wonder about something else." It was the first time anyone had ever called me "Sir," and although I didn't rate the title it made me feel good. "Now bugger off," I concluded. "I've got things to do."

"Yes, sir," Slater said again, and they vanished.

Feb. 10—We transited, as the expression goes, the Canal today, and while it's interesting once it's nothing I'd want to do for a living. The transit is tricky enough so that every ship has to carry a Canal pilot, and the pilots are licensed for one direction only. They make the run, then take the train back to the starting point, where they rest up before making another transit. They are in complete command of your ship while they're aboard.

PCs are small enough so that they bunch them up with other boats in the same lock, and that way expedite matters to a certain degree. (One PC, nested astern of a banana boat, managed to ram the stern of the banana boat and knock its skipper tumbling out of the privy on the fantail, his trousers still around his ankles. They later painted a bunch of bananas on their bridge wing, in the spot saved for U-boat and airplane kills.)

At any rate, you start in at the Gatun locks, which take you up in three stages to the level of Gatun Lake, a large body of fresh water that gives everyone a chance to clean the salt off his decks and flush out his fire hoses. Then from Gatun Lake you run twenty-four miles eastward to Gamboa, where the Gaillard cut begins. This is an eight-mile stretch that was cut through the hills, and it's so narrow the jungle seems to be coming at you from both sides. Then the Pedro Miguel lock lets you down to within about fifty feet of sea level, and you cross a small lake to the two Miraflores locks, which let you down the rest of the way. After that it's a run of about eight miles to Balboa, and beyond that the Bay of Panama and the Pacific. The whole trip, from shore to shore, is only forty miles, but what with one thing and another it takes up the better part of a day. Also, because of the way the Isthmus squirms at that particular point, your transit from the Atlantic to the Pacific is on a generally north-south course, and you wind up at the Pacific end twenty-two miles east of the entrance at the Atlantic end. At one point, in the stretch from Gatun to Gamboa, you're even going on an east-northeast course. I throw that in for people who like to make bets in saloons.

We'll spend the night here at the base in Balboa, and then tomorrow we're off into the Pacific. For something I used to think about with terror, it now doesn't seem much different from anything else. But then I guess all big changes happen slowly, which is just as well because it gives us time to adjust. It's those sudden jolts that are bad for the nerves.

III · THE PACIFIC

March 30—We arrived in Pearl Harbor today, after what seems like thirty years at sea. From Panama we ran up the coast to San Diego, in company with another PC and a tanker that was running light, and this turns out to be a trip of some thirty-five hundred miles, which, when you're making eight knots, can take quite a while. Like eighteen days. We refueled and re-watered and re-everythinged in Dago, and then, with the same PC plus a PCE(R), which is a clumsy-looking rescue ship, we set out to escort a tug and tow to Pearl. This was only thirteen days, or practically overnight.

There are several ways the Pacific is different from the Atlantic, some of which are obvious right away and some of which take a while to notice. For one thing, the action of the waves is different; each wave that comes at you has been travelling over thousands of miles of open ocean, and it develops a long swell that seems to have a quality of its own. I don't know how to explain it better than that, but you can *feel* the distance behind each wave, and the sense of space surrounding it. And to tell where land is out here, you simply look for the nearest cumulus cloud. The heat rising off land condenses as it gets higher, so if you see a cumulus cloud surrounded by a lot of clear sky, the best bet is that it's hovering over an island. And if the cloud has a faint tinge of green along its underside, you know it's over a patch of jungle.

The matter of fresh water in the Pacific is one of the things a PC sailor notices first. A PC has one evaporator, which distils seawater into fresh, but it has to be taken apart and scaled every hundred hours, so it's used only in an emergency. In the Atlantic the trips were short enough so it didn't matter, but out here the water begins to run low after a few days, and we have to fill up. For this reason we always travel long distances in the company of a tug or someone else with plenty of water, and we also do everything we can to save water along the way. This means no showers, except when we're actually taking on water and can top off the tanks, and as a result there are times when the ship's company gets kind of gamey. So whenever it rains, or looks about to rain, the word is passed: "Get out the soap!" and everyone strips down to shower clogs, grabs a bar of soap, and runs for the foredeck. I'm here to state that nothing tastes sweeter than rainwater you catch in your open mouth, and nothing feels better than to have the soapsuds washed off you by water straight out of the sky.

Another effect of these longer trips is that those who've been used to hitting the bars between convoys find this sudden lack of booze leaves them with a craving for sweets. The old hands know about it, and fill their lockers with all sorts of pogey bait before we shove off, but the newcomers are left gnawing their knuckles and begging Caproni to make up a batch of sweet rolls, or pies, or anything with sugar.

The mail gets more important out here, and with long stretches of nothing to do the guys just sit around the mess hall and write. But it's hard to write to someone you haven't heard from in a long time, and pretty soon this frustration shows. I was trying to think of something witty to write Diane one day, when one of the snipes, who was sitting beside me, said, "See what you think of this," and pushed a letter across. I took it and read: "Dear Mom, Do you know what I am going to do. every time I get a letter from youse I'm going to send one back. that's the only time that youse are going to hear from me. so wise up." He looked at me questioningly, and I nodded and slid the letter back.

"That ought to do it," I said.

"You think she'll get it?" he asked.

"You know her better than I do," I replied. "She sure as hell ought to."

He re-read the letter, folded it, and slipped it into an envelope. "Some people need a little goose now and then," he said.

Napier, the Electrician's Mate, has a harder one to write. The last letter he got from his wife ended with the PS: "Am pregnant. Will explain later." He keeps staring at the letter and counting the time since his last leave, which was in July, and then he stares at the bulkhead for a long time, his pencil not quite touching the paper. He's started several letters and torn them up, because he says he doesn't want to jump to any conclusions until he's heard her explanation, but it's impossible for him to write about anything else because he can't *think* about anything else. "It's a hell of a thing," is all he says.

Coming into Pearl Harbor you'd never guess the damage the Japs did three years ago, and you have to look hard to see signs of the attack. There's that little platform around the mainmast of the sunken *Arizona*, where the colors are always at half staff, but that's just in Battleship Row and the base goes for miles in all directions. Every possible kind of ship is in here, from battleships to carriers to auxiliaries to cruisers to subs to tin cans to PCs to SCs, and the launches that criss-cross the harbor are as busy as water bugs. We went to the fuel dock and took on fuel and water, then were directed to nest outboard of two other PCs in a sort of out-of-the-way spot. That is it *looked* out-of-the-way, but we hadn't been there ten minutes before a launch pulled up and a Yeoman in crisp whites came aboard with a package of official mail. He had the faintly snotty attitude of all headquarters personnel, and gave the impression he was soiling his uniform by being aboard. We weren't what you'd call the sharpest-looking ship, after a month or so at sea, and our dungarees and work shirts had begun to fade from being washed on a line dragged astern then whip-dried in the wind, but we resented the Yeoman's attitude, and wondered how long he'd last under the tender leadership of Van Gelder, our Bosun's Mate First. There's a division between seagoing and shore-based personnel that goes through all levels of the fleet, with each side regarding the other with mild or not-so-mild contempt. We're irritated by the fact that the shore-based bastards have first call on all the girls, leaving us to scuff around among the castoffs and other debris, while they resent the fact that we have a chance to be heroes and even if we're not we sometimes act as though we were. It's all summed up best by the fact that the Base Officers' Club is known as just that, while the Fleet Officers' Club is known as the Monkey House. The enlisted men's names for each other aren't always that polite.

The official mail this page-boy delivered contained a number of surprises, some of them good and some bad, depending on where you sat. The first and most jarring surprise was that the captain is being relieved, and will be given command of a DE, while Mr. Taylor, who would normally have fleeted up to command, is being transferred to another DE as exec. A recent AlNav (bulletin for all Naval stations) promoted Mr. Taylor to full Lieutenant and Mr. Murray to Lieutenant (junior grade), so now Mr. Murray will be exec of our ship under the new captain, whose name is Rollins. We'll also get a new Ensign, a faceless number named Chilton, to fill out the complement. This is some big stirring up, leaving us with only one officer from the original ship's company, and we'll miss the captain and Mr. Taylor more than we'd like to say. We've known the captain since he was Mr. Ferguson, and to many of us he's become a part of the ship. But the Bureau figures a person can have command of a PC for only six months before he starts showing the strain, so they keep rotating to keep them fresh. Also, any officer over thirty is transferred out of PCs, but none of these rules seem to apply to enlisted men. I met a Gunner's Mate in Panama who was thirty-five years old and had been thirty-six months on the same PC. He was a little crazy.

Looking at the bright side of things we've at least got Mr. Murray as exec instead of Mr. Campbell, and that's about all I can say.

March 31—Another surprise today, this one a jim-dandy. Around noon a launch pulled alongside, and out of it climbed an Ensign and five enlisted men, all either Radiomen or Signalmen. The Ensign asked to see the captain, and Bessinger, who had the gangway watch, took him to the wardroom. I was standing nearby, and one of the Radiomen, a gangling clown with buck teeth, said, "Where do we stow our gear?"

"You better ask Altschuhl," I replied. "He's leading Radioman." I looked at the Signalmen, who seemed disinterested.

"We ain't part of your crew," the Radioman replied. "We're under Mr. Gonnick. We're the Control team."

"The—?" I didn't understand.

"Control team, mate. Communications Control."

"What do you do?"

"Ain't you heard?" He grinned, showing a line of teeth that looked like old tombstones. "We do invasions. That's our specialty dee la maysong."

"Oh." I swallowed. "Well—I don't know where you go. I guess the captain will know. He'll tell you where to bunk."

"He don't tell us nothing. Mr. Gonnick's our officer, and we don't take orders from nobody but him."

"Then what the hell are you asking me for?" I replied, and walked away. As I went down to the mess hall it came to me that in slightly under two days the ship had changed completely. From the sort of silly bucket we'd splashed around in a short while ago it was turning into a ship full of strangers, headed for the invasion of God knows what island. We'd heard that in February the Marines had landed on a small volcanic island called Iwo Jima, which had taken almost a month and thousands of casualties to secure, and any thoughts I'd had about a mail run in the Solomons were clearly out of the question. It would have been one thing if we still had the original ship's company, but with every day more newcomers came aboard, and with them the ship began to change its personality. It brought us oldtimers closer together, and even kids like Leemy and Slater were reassuring to have around. Needless to say, they clung to me like burrs to your socks.

April 1—Easter Sunday, for what that may be worth. Now we've invaded Okinawa, an island just to the south of the main Japanese islands. The boys on that invasion are probably going to take a terrible pasting, because the Japs can fly at them in relays from home base, and also reinforce the place whenever they want. I'm taking a personal interest in invasions these days; they no longer seem as far away as they used to, and I find myself looking for pictures or reports of PCs in the published accounts. There was one air shot, for instance, of the whole invasion line at Iwo Jima, and it was easy to pick out the PCs on their station just offshore. (That, it seems, is the reason for our five-mile bullhorn; the Control officer can call the LCVPs and other invasion barges and get them in the proper order before they start in. The timing is the most important part, because first there's a shore bombardment, then planes make strafing runs, then the idea is for the barges to hit the beach just after the strafing stops and before the Japs have a chance to get their heads up. Too early and we're hitting our own people; too late and we're giving the Japs a lot of nice, fat targets. I learn something new every day.)

April 2—Mr. Rollins, the new captain, came aboard today. He's a full Lieutenant, and one look at the fruit salad on his jacket shows he's been around a while. He has the pre-Pearl Harbor and American Theatre ribbons, and his Pacific ribbon has three battle stars. He's also wearing a red ribbon, with a thin blue-and-white stripe in the middle and a battle star, and this turns out to be the Philippine Liberation ribbon, meaning he took part in the

Leyte Gulf operation. Aside from his ribbons, his face shows that he's been around; he has the quiet, no-nonsense approach you see in combat veterans, and his skin underneath the suntan has the yellowish tinge that comes from taking Atabrine. (Atabrine, which we had to use as a substitute when the Japs captured all the quinine supply, keeps off malaria but also turns you a sickly yellow. Everybody who was in the South Pacific turned that color, and the only cure was to keep up a good suntan. When you lost that, you began to look like a canary.) Mr. Rollins is quiet, as I've said, but I think he's probably all right. He's going to have to be, taking over from Mr. Ferguson.

The new Ensign, Mr. Chilton, is something else again. He's a big, rangy guy, with white teeth, a deep suntan, and lots of muscle, and there's something about him that reminds me of Mr. Campbell except I don't think he's as bright as Mr. Campbell was. It turns out he was what's called a Tunney Fish, a physical ed specialist in a program run by Comdr. Gene Tunney, the former boxer, and he was a Chief who got turned into an Ensign. He is, needless to say, an exercise nut; he brought a set of bar bells with him, and he put up a cot on the signal bridge because he says he can't sleep below. The captain shrugged, since it's going to be Mr. Rollins' problem, but I got the picture that on *his* ship Mr. Chilton would damn well sleep with the others.

April 3—The captain showed Mr. Rollins around the ship, put us through general drills, and then started signing the logs and other papers for the transfer. Late this afternoon we got into our whites and were mustered aft, and there were the usual readings of orders and speeches we couldn't hear because of the generator noise. I'd liked to have heard what Mr. Ferguson said but it wasn't hard to get the idea, and to a lot of us it felt as though we were losing a member of the family. Then Mr. Ferguson and Mr. Taylor said goodbye informally to us all, and we put the outboard motorboat over the side and they went ashore. The ship looked different the moment they left.

The captain—Mr. Rollins—was aware of how we felt, and didn't do anything to so to speak rock the boat. He's making no changes right now, and he's doing nothing that might cause resentment. He's nobody's fool, which is good to know. He's also dealt with Communications Control teams before, and if Mr. Gonnick's boys think they're going to get away with anything they've got another think coming. Mr. Gonnick may be their officer, but that doesn't mean they can do as they please. The first time they talked, the captain saw to it that Mr. Gonnick understood that.

April 15—We've been at sea nearly a week, running alone at fifteen knots, and in a day or so we should hit Eniwetok. I say "nearly" a week because I've begun to lose all sense of time. In the Atlantic we went from one port to another on a regular schedule; here the distances are such that you're either at sea or you're not, and that's all you know. You get numb to the passage of time, and one day is like the one before it which was like the one before that. Also, somewhere along the way we crossed the International Date Line, but all that meant was that instead of being Tuesday it was suddenly Wednesday (or whatever), and the only place where that made any difference was in the log.

Eniwetok is a small coral atoll in the Marshall Islands, which was retaken from the Japs a year ago February, when we started our island-hopping campaign. They tell me there's nothing there but a lagoon and an airstrip, but at least it's a place where we can get fuel and water. We might even be able to take a swim, if conditions are right.

Speaking of the island-hopping campaign, a little while ago we passed (but didn't see) the island of Wotje, which is still inhabited by Japs. It's one of those islands we decided weren't worth invading, and the Japs, who know a bargain when they see one, don't do anything to bring themselves to our attention. It's a funny feeling, though, to know that just over the horizon are all those Japs, and every now and then I have an urge to turn around and look astern, to see if anything's following. I suppose it's a feeling I'll get over, given time.

Of course the big news, a couple of days ago, was the death of President Roosevelt. I don't remember anyone else being President, and it's certainly going to sound funny to say "President Truman." Who this Truman is or what he's like no one seems to know, but my feeling is it couldn't have happened at a worse time. I'm glad I don't have *his* job.

April something—I don't know what the date is, and I don't care. I particularly don't want to write this, but I suppose I have to. I wish to God . . . well, there's no point wishing.

We fueled and took on water at Eniwetok, then anchored in the lagoon for the night. It was a usual Pacific day, with just a few clouds on the horizon, and when Van Gelder asked the captain if we could get up a swimming party the captain said sure, so long as the usual routine was observed. So the heads were secured, and one man—Lindquist— went to the flying bridge with a rifle and binoculars, to act as shark watch. Then everybody peeled off their clothes and dove over the side, and I don't think any water ever felt so good. We clowned around, we swam under the ship, and we dove off the flying bridge (the captain vetoed

Humma's request to dive from the crow's nest), and for a while we were all kids again, splashing and spraying and laughing at nothing in particular. Then, one by one, people began to climb back aboard, and I noticed that the sky had suddenly turned dark. I pulled myself up onto the screw guard and felt how cold the wind had become, and saw a squall racing toward us. Lindquist shouted at those who'd swum farthest away to come back, and there were still six or seven in the water when the squall struck. It was as though someone had turned a switch; the light went out and the wind shrieked, and whitecaps appeared and rolled before the wind like surf. I heard someone shouting and saw him point, and when I looked I saw a small dot against the white of the waves. An arm reached up, and waved frantically.

"Who is it?" I asked.

"Pin-Head!" said one of the snipes. "Christ, he's gone!"

Sometimes you do things without thinking, and before I knew it I found myself in the water, swimming as hard as I could. I didn't know what I was going to do when I reached him; my only thought was to get there as fast as possible. I did, after what seemed like a half hour, and I could see he was practically gone. His eyes were wide and water was coming from his nose and mouth, and he was struggling wildly to keep from going under. I managed to get an arm around him, and then saw that the wind was carrying us both toward the line of surf that stretched across the entrance to the lagoon. Nothing I did could change it; all I could do was keep Pin-Head's face above water until we were boiled in the surf or taken out to sea. I was just starting to curse myself for a damned fool when the bow of a launch appeared over my head; a man got his hand under my armpit, and while someone else held Pin-Head I was yanked into the launch like a giant tuna. Then they brought Pin-Head in, and he lay limply over a thwart while they pounded the water out of him. The boat crew wore kapok lifejackets, which made them look like stuffed animals. The launch, which reared like a horse in the wind-driven sea, headed around toward a destroyer that was keeping its searchlight on us.

Faintly, to one side, I saw a blinking light and recognized Leemy's halting signal rhythm, and he was sending the words "One more." He repeated it, and I clawed my way back to the officer in charge of the boat. He was an Ensign; he'd lost his cap, and his hair was plastered wetly to his forehead.

"There's another one!" I shouted. "One more!" He frowned, and I pointed to where Leemy was sending the words again, then he said something under his breath and pulled the launch around. The destroyer's searchlight skittered back and forth across the water, looking for another head, but all anyone could see was white foam in the darkness, and pretty soon we gave up. By now, anyone who'd been in the water was either under the surface or had been taken out to sea. We went back to the destroyer, where Pin-Head and I were helped aboard, both of us shivering and naked as jay birds. After a PC, a destroyer seemed as big as a battleship, and the ship's company all looked like professionals. They gave us dungarees and hot coffee, which helped, but I couldn't get my mind from the "One more" message, and I wondered if it'd been a mistake or if there really had been a third man in the water. I asked one of the men if I could send a message over to our ship to find out, and he said I'd have to ask the captain, who wanted to see us anyway.

We were taken down to the wardroom, where we met the

captain and several other officers (there are twenty-one of them on a can like this), and after I'd thanked the captain I asked him if I could use a light to call our ship. He said he'd have a Signalman do it, and I was about to say that *I* was a Signalman when something told me to shut up. I said, "Thank you, sir," and as we were about to leave the Medical Officer spoke up. Pin-Head was still trembling, and blue around the lips, and the doctor stopped him with a gesture.

"Wait a minute, there, son," he said. "How do you feel?"

"A little drag-ass," Pin-Head replied, then quickly added, "Sir."

"Hold on." The doctor vanished through a green curtain, and reappeared in a minute with a bottle of brandy. "Take this," he said, pouring a finger of liquor into a tumbler and handing it to Pin-Head. He poured another and gave it to me, saying, "It won't do you any harm, either."

"Doc, you're going to have these men cockeyed," the captain told him. "They look like beer drinkers to me."

"Time they learned about life," the doctor replied, slapping the cork back into the bottle. "Got to get their circulation going."

I tried to take my brandy in one gulp, but it caught in my throat and I almost strangled. I finally managed to get it down, and wheezingly thanked the captain again, trying not to notice the smile on his face. Pin-Head had tossed his drink back with no trouble, and his lips began to look a little less blue.

The squall had passed when we got topside, leaving just a leaden sky overhead and a streak of lemon-yellow light along the horizon. The deck officer took us to the bridge, where he told a Signalman to get the PC on the light and find out what we wanted to know. We gave him our names, and when he'd got Leemy to come in with a "K" he sent: "Have Gillis and Bowers aboard. Was there anyone else?" Leemy's reply was short, and to the point.

"Gibbon," he sent.

I stared at the outline of our ship, unable to believe what I'd just seen, and I was about to ask the Signalman to get a repeat when I realized there was no point. The message would be the same, and the only trouble lay in my being able to believe it.

"Who is it?" Pin-Head asked.

I shook my head, and said, "Gib," then leaned over the rail and was sick.

We found out, when we got back to the ship, that Gibbon had jumped into the water shortly after I did, with some kind of idea of helping me. The poor crazy bastard, who couldn't blow his nose without getting into trouble, thought he could be some help to me even though he wasn't a very good swimmer. (I remembered, when he'd fallen over the side while fishing for red snapper, that he'd swum back to the screw guard with a strangely strangled kind of stroke, which used up a lot of energy without getting him very far.) The whole ship was plunged in black gloom, and every now and then someone would look over the side, or out toward the coral reef, in the hope of seeing something, but there never was anything there. Just the ships, riding quietly at anchor, and the line of surf along the opening.

We stayed in Eniwetok an extra couple of days, hoping that some sort of evidence would show up, but there was nothing, and we finally got underway. We went out the narrow channel through the surf, watching the waves curl past on either side of us, and I don't think there was a man topside who wasn't staring at the water as though to see beneath it. The captain realized he had what could turn into a bad situation here, with morale collapsing and everyone turning morbid, so as soon as we were squared away on our course for Guam he started running general drills, and we drilled until we were so tired we could barely stand. Then he came on the bullhorn and announced that, as of now, there would be no surprise GQ drills; any time the alarm rang without warning we could assume it was the real thing. This was a good idea, because it's an awful letdown to run like hell for your battle station, get all strapped in and ready to go, and then be told it's only a drill. You can see the look in the guys' eyes as they start to re-stow their gear, and it's the old thing of crying wolf. It's nice to know this captain doesn't believe in it.

The GQ alarm went off about eleven o'clock next morning, and if I had to guess I'd say that all stations were manned and ready in forty-five seconds. I've never seen the crew move so fast, and it turned out that what had caused the alarm was a floating mine, which a lookout spotted off the starboard bow. It was black, and you could see the top half of the round casing with the horns spiking out at all angles, and there was something about it that reminded me of a gigantic spider, lying in wait. The horns are glass tipped, and if they're hit they set off an impulse that detonates the mine, and while by international law all mines are supposed to go on safe if they break loose from their moorings, this isn't anything you can rely on, as we were soon to see. It just bobbed there, black and ugly, and we approached it gingerly, until it was about three hundred yards away. (It's dangerous to come closer than two hundred yards, because if you should detonate it pieces of the casing could fly out and mangle someone.)

The most inexperienced of the gunners were those on the new 20-millimeters—the ones that replaced the forward K-guns—so the captain let them have first crack at the mine. Each gun fired a full magazine, but they were so low down and close to the water that they were firing almost parallel to the surface, and all they did was kick up a lot of spray and send ricochets winging off in all directions. Then we circled a little closer, and it was Bessinger's turn. (My GQ station was now signals, so he had a Seaman loader.) He had a better angle of fire, and he was churning up a fountain of spray when suddenly BLAM! there was a flash of orange-yellow light, water and pieces of mine casing flew through the air and splashed back like hail, and then there was only smoke hanging over the quivering sea. Lincoln, on the flying-bridge 20-millimeter, stared at the spot with eyes as large as turkey eggs, and finally whispered, "Man! I never did see anything like *that*!"

We secured from GQ and Lincoln went up to the crow's nest, where he spent the rest of the day. Green finally got him down to help serve lunch, but he went right back again afterward, saying he was getting as far from the surface of the water as possible. "Hell, man, a thing like that could sink us in nothing flat," he said. "I aim to be up where I can jump clear."

April 27—We're in Port Apra, Guam, which is a big fleet anchorage and just about the hottest spot you can imagine. It's maybe 110° in the shade and 130° in the sun, and for some reason the slight wind that comes off the water doesn't do much good. You go to one of the recreation areas on the beach, and you have a beer, and pretty soon the whole twelve ounces of beer come squirting out your forehead in the form of sweat. I saw a Bosun's Mate who claimed he could fill an empty beer can with sweat just by crooking his elbow over it and letting the water drip in while he drank beer with the other hand, and although I didn't stay to see the can filled I've no doubt he did it. He was a big, beefy man, and probably 98% water anyway. They say the human body is more water than anything else, and anyone who doubts it should come to Guam. You practically dissolve before your own very eyes.

Guam was retaken about a year ago, and every now and then you still see remains of the Jap bunkers. They're just holes in the ground, and a lot of twisted corrugated iron, but they offer some protection from the sun. Get a beer, and a can of peanuts, and you can almost pretend you're in a nightclub. You'll notice I said almost. And speaking of retaking Guam, Mr. Gonnick, our Control officer, was a landing-barge officer on that operation. There was a hidden reef off the beach, and the Japs, knowing the barges would stick on that reef, zeroed in a couple of 75-millimeter guns on the spot. The barges did get hung up, and the 75s banged them to pieces, and Mr. Gonnick had to swim. Yet, to look at him, you'd never think he'd done anything more dangerous than take a swim at the Y.

An armed messenger came aboard today, bringing a package of classified mail. Mr. Potter signed for it and then, since he's Communications Officer, he opened it and began to enter the various items in his log. (The captain was over on the beach, or he'd have got the stuff first.) One was a thick book, marked "Secret," and it was the Organization Book of the Pacific Fleet. Mr. Potter riffled through it, checking references back and forth, and finally said, "Well, well. I've always wanted to visit the colorful Orient."

Caulkins and I had been sitting on Caulkins' desk, wondering what we could write to Gibbon's family, and our ears perked up. "What's that, sir?" Caulkins asked. "A travel folder?"

"In a way," Mr. Potter replied. "Look here."

We went and looked over his shoulder, as he opened to a page of PCs, and he ran his finger down the line until he came to 1208. There was a code number after each ship, and he marked ours and then flipped to the forward part of the book. Our code number turned out to be "Forward Area, Central Pacific."

"Now get this," Mr. Potter said, and flipped to an area map, showing the various zones into which the Pacific was divided. There were exactly four bodies of land in the Forward Area, Central Pacific, and they were Honshu, Kyushu, Shikoku, and Hokkaido—the Japanese home islands. We stared at the map for a few moments, and I felt my mouth go dry. Mr. Potter looked at us, and smiled. "Better order your kimonos while you still have time," he said. "I hear the Japanese are sticklers for the proper dress." I tried to smile, but I don't think it was very convincing.

And, on the general subject of invasions, the word is that everything has hit the fan on Okinawa. The Japs are using the suicide tactics they developed at Leyte, and they're simply beating the hell out of our ships. They come in waves, so thick you can't shoot all of them down, and each plane is a flying bomb. The pilots are determined to die for their Emperor so there's no scaring them off—they must be drugged, or drunk, or something—and the only thing you can do is turn and twist and throw all the crap in the air you can, and just hope. PCs, of course, don't make as good targets as carriers, cans, and the rest, but that's a cold kind of comfort. A kamikaze pilot would just as soon hit a PC if nothing better was around.

Kamikaze, the name they use, means "Divine Wind," and it refers back to the thirteenth century, when a divine wind in the form of a typhoon broke up an invasion fleet of Kublai Khan's that was headed for Japan. (I got this indirectly from the captain, who was filling Mr. Murray in on the Leyte operation.)

May 8—It came over the Armed Forces radio today that Hitler is dead, and Gen. Jodl has signed the surrender of all German forces in Europe. This will be technically known as V-E, or Victory in Europe, Day, and I suppose there's a lot of celebration going on back Stateside. The Germans began surrendering May 4, so the whole thing is no great surprise, and as far as we out here are concerned it's just another day. It's nice that the Germans are through, but when you think of the Forward Area, Central Pacific, their importance looms very small. Mr. Potter typed up a note, which he put on the clipboard at the gangway watch station, and it read: "Germans will now be allowed on board ship, on payment of a 25¢ Visitors' Fee and a promise of good behavior." When the captain saw it he thought a minute, and those of us who were watching held our breaths.

"Make the bastards pay a dollar," he said, and went below.

May 10—We've developed a blow-by in one of our main Diesels, which fills the engine room with smoke and results in a loss of power, so we're stuck here in Guam until we can get it fixed. This, considering what's happening further west, is perfectly all right with me. Guam may not be Times Square, but at least you don't have crazy Japanese diving planes at you all day.

A replacement, if you could call him that, for Gibbon came aboard today. He's a Seaman named Treadway, and he's one of the first of the draftees to be accepted by the Navy (up until now we've all been volunteer). I can tell already that he's a whiner, and a goldbrick, and he's going to have one piss-poor time on this ship if he doesn't shape up. It'll be interesting to see what a few weeks with Van Gelder will do for him.

June 6—We're now between Guam and Okinawa, in company with the PCE(R) and a tug that's towing pre-fabricated sections of a pier. It's slow going, because the tug can't make any better than six knots, and we have to zigzag all over the place to stay with it. (Our dead-slow speed, on one engine, is about eight, and when we took on water from the tug we had to tow a couple of GI garbage cans astern to slow us down.) Early this afternoon, when Mr. Potter had the deck, the captain and Mr. Murray were in the wardroom playing cribbage, and Mr. Chilton was sacked out on his cot on the signal bridge, the sonar picked up a nice, sharp echo, with down-Doppler that showed it was moving away. Mr. Potter checked the bearing to make sure there was nothing on the surface, then called the captain on the intercom, and the minute the captain heard the echo he sounded GQ. He told me to break out the contact pennant, which is a black streamer about ten feet long, and to signal the tug to make an emergency left turn to avoid depth charges (the contact was directly in front of the tug). We came up to attack speed, ran in, and dropped a quick pattern of shallow charges, then circled around the tug to regain contact. The water thundered and leaped with the explosions, and the deck plates stung our feet, and in a few moments we had the contact again, astern of the tow.

This time the captain decided on a mousetrap attack, which is more accurate than the depth charges, so he ordered the racks loaded and the safety wires removed. Some of the guys had washed their dungarees and hung them on the bow lifelines to dry, but there was no chance to remove them now, and when the mousetrap charges went off the dungarees were incinerated by the blast, with only the belt loops remaining when the smoke cleared. The projectiles sailed out and dropped into the water far ahead, but there was no sound of an explosion, so we knew they'd missed. We made one more mousetrap attack with the same result, and then changed back to depth charges when one of the mousetrap racks began to misfunction. We made two depth-charge attacks, and were starting the run for the third when the depth-charge station called to say they'd run out of charges and would have to hoist more up from the magazine. It was a beautiful contact, sharp and clear, with pronounced down-Doppler.

To use the time until the charges were brought up, the captain got a range on the contact, then turned the sonar from pinging to listening, and for thirty seconds listened for screw noises. But there was total silence, and when he turned the sonar back to pinging he got the contact right off, five hundred yards farther away than before. This meant it was going at a rate of half-a-mile a minute, or thirty knots, and anything that made that kind of speed without screw noises had to be a fish, most likely a whale. (The average speed of a submerged sub is from three to five knots.) But why we hadn't hit it, or at least brought up some evidence of damage, was a mystery. For a while the captain stared at the chemical recorder, the device that gives the proper time to fire both depth charges and mousetraps. He looked at the traces made by the stylus, which were so precise they looked like a textbook illustration.

"Mr. Murray," he said, at last, "when was this recorder last zeroed?" (The machine should be checked every now and then, and adjusted in accordance with the electrical power, the water temperature, the air temperature, and a few other factors.)

"Uh—I'm not quite sure, sir," Mr. Murray said. "A while ago, I guess."

"Since you've been in the Pacific?"

"Uh—no, sir. I don't imagine so."

"Let's do it now, should we?"

"Yes, sir."

They got the readings and made the tests, and it turned out that the recorder was off enough to have made every pattern miss by fifty yards. There was dead silence in the wheel house, and the captain licked his lips.

"That was some lucky whale," he said, quietly. "Secure from General Quarters."

By now the tug and the PCE(R) were almost over the horizon, and it was getting dark when we caught up with them. The recorder wasn't mentioned again.

June 10—We should be in Okinawa tomorrow, and while things have quieted down somewhat it still isn't a place you'd come for a rest cure.

Two things worth mentioning happened on the way: A few days ago we saw a tug headed eastward, towing something that looked like a big, triangular house. The captain had me blink over and ask what he had there, and the reply came: "A suburb of Pittsburgh." The captain thought a moment, then laughed, and explained that the cruiser

Pittsburgh had had her bow torn off in a typhoon (the season has already begun), and that this must be what it was. We'd earlier seen the *Pittsburgh*, minus her bow, in Guam.

Then yesterday Lincoln, who was sitting in the crow's nest, gave a loud holler of "Aircraft!" and we all scurried around and looked at the sky, but could see nothing. But he kept pointing at something, and finally, by using his binoculars and standing in the shade of a gun mount, the captain saw it. It was the planet Venus which Lincoln, through some kind of superhuman concentration, had been able to pick out of the whole bright blue sky. One by one the rest of us saw it, and Linkovitch confirmed it with the help of the Rude Star Finder, which we use for navigation. With eyesight like that, Lincoln ought to be made permanent lookout.

The sunset tonight was kind of spooky. We're close enough to Okinawa so the dust of battle hangs in the air over the horizon, and while you can't see it in the daytime it filters the rays of the setting sun into odd designs. Tonight, just after the sun had set, long ribbons of red fanned out into the sky, looking exactly like the rays on the Japanese battle flag. Aside from being weird to look at it also seemed like a sort of omen, and not a particularly good one. I remember a story Miss Gresham gave us in school—it was a condensed version, not the whole thing—about an Anglo-Saxon hero named Beowulf, who killed the monster Grendel and then went to Grendel's mother's underwater cave to kill her (she was a real mean old bitch), and for a moment tonight I had the feeling that we're approaching the lair of some monster that lurks under water. I'll be glad when daylight comes.

June 11—Today we saw where the smoke and dust are

coming from. The northern half of the island was secured fairly early, but the Japs set up a line in the south, and are dug in good and solid. They're hidden in bunkers and caves, and the Marines have to flush them out with explosives and flame throwers, or, if that doesn't work, they dynamite the entrance and seal the whole business off. No matter how they do it there's a lot of exploding going on, and the air is full of dust and other debris.

We delivered our tug to Buckner Bay, formerly known as Nakagasuku Wan, and when we reported to the command ship we were given an anchorage and told to await further orders. The captain, on advice from a PC skipper who's been here a while, anchored astern of an LST that has smoke generators; we don't carry them, and this friend pointed out it's good to be near a smoke ship at night, for protection against kamikazes. Apparently they come over at all hours of the day and night, and dump themselves into whatever shipping they can see. For this reason we're not supposed to fire unless we're absolutely certain they've seen us, because once we start firing all the pilot has to do is run down the line of our tracers, and bang. (We heard of one brilliant man who set up a couple of 20-millimeters with remote control on a pile of rocks at Kerama Retto, off the southwestern part of the island, and when the planes came over at night he squeezed off a few rounds and fooled them into diving onto the rocks. For a while, it worked like a charm.)

June 12—We had our first air raid last night, and I must say it wasn't what I expected. Along about eleven o'clock the radio announced a Flash Yellow, which meant that planes were approaching the area, and about ten minutes later came a Flash Red, meaning they were headed for us. We came to GQ and just sort of stood there, wearing our

163

helmets and lifejackets, while the ships around us made smoke. The smoke smells of a combination of charcoal and tin; it makes a big, white cloud but it doesn't choke you, and it's more like a good, pea-soup fog than anything else. Of course the ship ahead of us couldn't get its generators going, so we had a big spot of open sky above us, but no planes appeared, and all we saw were the stars. Planes appeared at other places, however; we heard radio reports of two that crashed into exposed ships, but there was no word of damage so we didn't know any more. Then the Flash Green was announced, and we secured.

I noticed one strange thing as we came to GQ, and that was a number of small lights in the hills surrounding the harbor. I mentioned it to the captain, and he said they were made by Japs, who were still hiding in caves and who came out whenever there was a raid and lit beacon lights to guide their planes. You've got to say one thing for them— they're always in there pitching.

July 1—All "organized" resistance stopped on June 21, and today the island is officially secured—that is, it's no longer an automatic battle star just to be here. But today is pretty much like any day in the last two weeks; we've been doing odd jobs such as night picket duty, escorting ships to and from the small nearby islands, and just generally hacking around. None of it is what you'd call exactly habit-forming, and some of it is scary as all hell.

We saw a DE, for instance, that was jumped by five kamikazes at one time, and he didn't seem to have a snowball's chance of surviving. But then one of the kamikazes hit the water short of the ship, a second they caught with their 5-inch guns, the third lit back in their depth charges but for some reason didn't explode them, the fourth missed the bridge and piled into the water beyond, and the

164

fifth, which was headed straight down the stack, was blown apart by a Marine in a Corsair, who followed him down through all the flak and chopped him up before he could hit the ship. The Marine then zoomed up, waggled his wings, and flew off.

(A switch on the kamikaze plane is a piloted, manned bomb called a baka bomb—baka means "idiot"—which is carried under a regular plane and then launched near the target. It has stubby control surfaces, just enough to aim it where it wants to go.)

We didn't see, but we heard about, an SC that had a kamikaze come right for the bridge, and just before it seemed about to hit, the skipper jumped over the side (who can blame him?). But the kamikaze missed; nobody else had jumped, and the exec had to bring the ship around and pick up the swimming captain. As far as that ship went he was dead, and he had to ask for transfer somewhere else.

We did see, and weren't much cheered by, a burned-out PG being towed back from Kerama Retto. A PG is a PC converted into a gunboat, with supposedly enough fire-power to take care of itself, but this one had come off a poor second, and all that remained was the blackened hulk. Nobody looked at it for very long; one quick glance was all you needed.

Another non-cheerful sight, but only when you thought about it, were the occasional big, fat flies we found aboard ship. We were going along the coast one day, and saw a C-47 hedge-hopping a few feet off the ground, trailing a cloud of spray behind it. Mr. Gonnick explained it was disinfectant, because of all the unburied bodies and the flies they attracted, and it was then we realized the meaning of the fat flies we'd been seeing—they were carrion flies, come out from the beach for a change of air. They weren't hard to kill, because they were so sluggish.

We did see one sort of pleasant thing, but Pin-Head and I were probably the only ones who really appreciated it. We were on picket duty one night with a full moon, and our station was maybe five miles off the beach, within sight of the anchorage. The radio announced a Flash Red, and slowly, where the ships had been, fog began to take their place until they were out of sight, and the whole scene looked like a moonlight view of Nantucket from Altar Rock. No planes appeared—or if they did, they couldn't find any target—and after a while Flash Green was called, and within a half hour the fog had drifted away and we could see the ships again. During the time the alert had been on the anchorage was, to my mind, a fog pocket on the moors, and for the first time in a long while I was homesick. I thought about Diane, and thought of other and better ways to play my cards next time I saw her, and for a while Okinawa might as well not have existed.

July 16—We're in a convoy underway for the Philippines, where we'll stage for the invasion of you-know-what.

In spite of the fact that Okinawa is supposed to be secure, the last couple of weeks have been anything but restful. The kamikazes still come over at night (one dumped himself onto the fantail of the *Tennessee*, and did considerable damage), and the Japs in the hills still light their signal fires, so the word "secure" just means we're not about to be thrown off. We're in business, but we still have to be careful.

Then there are the typhoons. About every five days one of them forms up, back around Guam, and starts off on a generally westward course that can take it any number of places. Some of them recurve to the north, some

tossed and heaved, and we rolled so far over you could hear everything loose below decks go tumbling back and forth, while the wind screeched in the rigging and the ship shuddered every time the screws came out of water. When, finally, some sort of visibility returned, our LSTs were scattered all over the ocean, and it took us another day to round them up. The seas were still mountainous, but at least you could hear yourself above the wind, and Caproni was able to put together some sandwiches. During the worst of the storm you ate what you could grab in one hand, while you hung on with the other. Treadway, the draftee, was so paralyzed with fear and seasickness we thought for a while he'd died, but he'd just sort of passed out. With him, it doesn't make much difference one way or the other.

So here we are now in this convoy, which is like no other convoy because there are more escorts than ships being escorted. Apparently Operations kept us all around Okinawa until there were enough to make into a group, so we've got eight LSTs being escorted by nine ships: The DE *Underhill* is escort commander, and the rest are PCs, SCs, and our old faithful PCE(R). Normally the ratio is three escorts to a dozen or more ships, and this imbalance has made us all feel a little silly. As we filed out of Buckner Bay this afternoon the sun was shining, we were leaving the combat area, and among the crew there was a good deal of horsing around. Robbins had rigged a CO_2 bottle as a Coke dispenser and was spraying people with it, Bessinger and Lindquist were Indian wrestling in the 40-millimeter gun tub, and Van Gelder was showing two seamen how to rig a punching bag on the stack. (Lincoln, as usual, was in the crow's nest.) In the wardroom Mr. Murray and Mr. Potter were playing cribbage, Mr. Chilton was doing push-ups on the signal bridge, and Mr. Donath was making peanut-butter fudge in the wardroom pantry. The captain, on the flying bridge, watched Okinawa dwindle astern with no visible regret. He usually throws a penny over the side as we leave a harbor, for good luck and to ensure a safe return, but this time he said he was damned if he wanted to come back to Okinawa, so he didn't throw anything. I hope he doesn't have cause to regret it; everybody can always do with a little good luck.

The *Underhill* is a good ship. She's just out of the Atlantic, where she's been working with a hunter-killer group, and her men are sharp and morale is high. We could tell that when we went alongside to pass her some charts, and just working with a ship like that makes you feel everything's going to be all right. You can tell it without even going on board: it radiates efficiency like a big, bright light.

July 25—Yesterday was a day I don't guess I'll ever forget. Our screen was an elaborate one, with one PC way out ahead as a scout, the PCE(R) bringing up the rear in case there was anyone to rescue, then the PCs and SCs in a ring around the convoy, with the *Underhill* in bow position. In the middle of the morning we got a radar contact off to port, range fourteen thousand yards; the *Underhill* got it, too, and ordered all escorts to close in to their anti-aircraft stations. We bunched closer to the convoy, and with our glasses could just barely see one aircraft in the distance, but it didn't get any closer and finally disappeared, so we went back to our normal screening stations. We felt a little disappointed that we hadn't been able to show the plane how good our gunnery was. (We'd been having anti-aircraft practice, with the *Underhill* throwing up shell bursts for us to shoot at, and felt we could knock down any plane that came near.)

When we were back on station, the captain went below and Mr. Potter took the deck (Mr. Chilton hasn't qualified to stand a watch yet, so he just lurks around and tries to pretend he's learning), and in a little while the DE opened up with his light. I took the message, which said, in part, "It occurs to me you people might like some ice cream. I will give five gallons of ice cream to three ships a day in the following order of rotation." It then listed the ships, and we were third in line. I took the message down and knocked on the wardroom door, and when the captain told me to come in Mr. Donath was saying, "I heard in Guam the birdmen have a pool the war will be over by October. They've got a million-dollar pool, and you can dip into it for any amount you want."

"Did they say October what year?" the captain asked, reading my message.

"I don't know," Mr. Donath replied. "All I heard was October."

"Listen to this," the captain said, and read the message about the ice cream. "I think that's pretty damn nice."

"I guess he's a nice guy," Mr. Donath said. He shuffled the cards, and dealt out two cribbage hands.

The captain initialed the message, and handed it back to me. "Just give him a Roger," he said. "And ask Caproni to come up to the wardroom."

I went back to the signal bridge, and after a few minutes I heard Caproni as he came running out of the wardroom. "Ice cream, you bastards!" he shouted. *Ice cream!*" He hurried aft, to look for some containers.

It was a fire-hot day, with the sea and sky a blazing blue, and the decks and railings burned to the touch. I was glad for the shade of the canvas awning I'd strung over the signal bridge, and I stood with my back to the mast and watched the first PC approach the *Underhill* for ice cream. Then the *Underhill* opened up with his light again, and I jumped for my light, turned the switch, and gave him a "K."

"Hold off on the ice cream," he sent. "Have spotted a mine, and am going to sink it."

I told Mr. Potter, who passed the word to the captain on the intercom, and then I took my spyglass and could see a small, black dot in the water ahead of the DE, and after a while little dashes of spray spurted up around it from the DE's 20-millimeters. The rest of the convoy came left to avoid the mine, and headed toward us. Mr. Potter notified the captain, who came up and took the conn, swinging us out to give the ships more room.

The intercom opened up with a sputter, and Altschuhl's voice, from the radio shack, said, "Tell the captain the DE says he's got a sub contact. He's leaving the mine to chase the contact."

The DE's silhouette changed as it altered course, and then it dropped quickly astern of the convoy. "Five will get you seven it's a whale," Mr. Potter said.

"It might even be our whale," the captain replied, with a sideways glance at Mr. Murray. "It's one of those things we'll never know." Mr. Murray said nothing, but I saw his ears get red.

"The DE says he's making a run now," came Altschuhl's voice.

By now the word had spread throughout the ship, and people began to appear on deck in various stages of undress. We saw the DE, about three miles astern of the convoy, start its run, and we saw the puffs of smoke from the K-guns and then the fountains of dirty gray water as the charges went off. From that distance there was no noise and very little movement; it was almost like a series of still pictures.

"DE says he thinks he got it," said Altschuhl's intercom.

"He sure uses his radio a lot," Mr. Donath observed.

"Doctrine," the captain replied. "That's what the book says you're supposed to do."

"I never knew anyone to follow the book like that, though," Mr. Potter put in. "He must be a trade-school boy. And I still bet it's a whale."

"He's just out of the Atlantic," the captain said. "He probably thinks every contact he gets is a sub."

"DE says he's got a sub on the surface," came the intercom. "He's chasing it and is going to ram." Altschuhl's voice showed a faint tinge of excitement.

We strained our eyes, but the *Underhill* was beginning to shimmer in the horizon heat waves, and she became hard to follow. Then there was a small burst of smoke, and I thought excitedly that she might have exploded the sub, but the smoke turned into a boil of orange flame and started to rise upward; it bubbled and boiled and churned in a curdling of orange and black until it got up to about ten thousand feet, and then the smoke flattened out and mushroomed dirtily into the base of some white cumulus clouds. The *Underhill* disappeared from sight. Around me I could hear the comments of the others:

"That was the DE blew up."

"Ke-rist, did she go!"

"There ain't no survivors there."

"Where's the DE?"

"She blew up."

"Jeeziz, lookit that smoke!"

"That's the DE, all right."

"There's nobody getting off that ship."

172

"The sombitch sure blew up."

"You can't see nothing but smoke."

The smoke lifted a bit from the horizon, and underneath it was a tiny spot that seemed to be spurting steam. It disappeared as I watched, and a lonely, hollow feeling came over me.

The intercom opened up, and everyone jumped. "Convoy commodore wants us to go back and look for survivors," Altschuhl said. "Us and the PCE(R)."

"Acknowledge," said the captain. "Sound General Quarters."

The GQ alarm honked throughout the ship as we swung around, came up to full speed, and headed back toward the base of the column of smoke. We could see that something was still floating there but we couldn't make it out, and we were all concentrating on the spot when Lincoln, on the flying-bridge 20-millimeter, screeched, "Sub on the starboard bow!" There, only a couple of hundred yards off, a small conning tower bobbed in the water, and what was visible of the sub beneath it made it look no longer than a torpedo. The captain started to swing toward it, then changed his mind.

"Target to starboard," he said. "All guns commence firing."

The 3-inch gun and the starboard 20-millimeters opened up with a hellish noise, and through the spray we could see the conning tower drift astern and sink slowly out of sight. I don't think we scored any hits because there were no explosions, but the sub was gone, and no longer a menace.

"Cease firing," the captain said, and then, to Mr. Gonnick, "You know what I think that was? I think it was a one-man sub—a piloted torpedo. He was trying to get us to ram him."

"Submarine port beam!" someone shouted, and we swung the guns around and blasted away until it, too, vanished.

"That's just what they are," Mr. Gonnick said. "And that's what the DE rammed. The little bastards."

The captain thought a moment. "They were probably left in our path by a mother sub," he began, just as Lincoln yelled, "Sub dead ahead!" The captain came hard left, and made a wide enough circle so that the 40-millimeter gun could be brought to bear, and this time we saw the flash of two explosions through the spray before the sub went down.

"As you were saying," Mr. Gonnick remarked, when we were back on course.

"And the mother sub was guided there by that plane this morning," the captain said. "The mine was a decoy, to get us to slow down."

There was silence for a few moments, then Mr. Gonnick said, "My God. Think what those could do to our line of departure."

"That's probably what they're practicing for," the captain replied. "They're getting the bugs out of the system, so's to be ready when we invade."

"Great," said Mr. Gonnick. "*That's* going to make for a merry Christmas."

"I hear we're scheduled to go in November first," said the captain. "Christmas may be a long way away."

"A long, long way," Mr. Gonnick agreed. "There's another, off to starboard."

We fired at this one, but it was so far off we couldn't see the results, and we kept on at full speed toward the remains of the *Underhill*. The PCE(R) and we arrived almost simultaneously, and we saw that the DE's bow, from the #1 gun forward, had drifted away, and the stern, from the stack aft, was floating quietly on the swells. The bridge portion, between the #1 gun and the stack, had just vanished—vaporized. As we got closer, we saw that the crew were still manning their guns; the 20-millimeter men were strapped in, and the 40-millimeter and other batteries were training back and forth, looking for a target. The men were stunned, and some of them smoke-blackened, but they were still a fighting ship. Those that were alive, that is; about half the ship's company had disappeared in the explosion, and there were a few dead and wounded on the decks, but all in all about a hundred and twenty had survived. The PCE(R), which was built for this kind of duty, took most of them off, while we circled around as a screen against any more midget subs. We saw some bodies in the water, but already the sharks were at work, and there wasn't much worth picking up.

There was a liferaft a short distance away, with three men in it, and we went over and brought them aboard. One was badly burned, but still in shock so there was no pain yet, and the other two acted like zombies. One just stared straight ahead and said nothing, while the other was kind of slack-jawed and could say only, "The whole world blew up. Everything. The whole goddam world." Considering what the explosion had looked like from several miles away, I could understand his feeling.

The PCE(R) and we took our survivors back to the convoy and put them aboard an LST, where there was a doctor and facilities to take care of them, and it was then we noticed that one of the SCs had broken down, and had to be taken in tow. One of the PCs was off chasing what it thought was the mother sub, so what had started as a screen of nine ships around the convoy was now reduced to three, and it was a real Chinese fire drill. Ships were going in all directions, some zigzagging and some patrolling and some chasing phantom contacts, while the convoy commodore tried desperately to restore order. He sent the PCE(R) and us back to sink the remains of the *Underhill*, which were a menace to navigation, and we spent most of the afternoon pumping 3-inch and 40-millimeter ammunition into that ship. But it had been so efficiently buttoned up that it took a long time to sink, and it was getting dark by the time the after section finally sloshed beneath the surface.

We then secured from GQ and headed back for the convoy, and when I looked astern I could still see the dark mushroom of smoke from the *Underhill*. It hung in the sky until the last pink streaks of afterglow were blotted out by the night.

Aug. 2—We arrived in Leyte Gulf today. It covers about a hundred square miles and there must be 500 ships here—battleships, carriers, cruisers, destroyers, attack transports, cargo ships, auxiliaries, minesweepers, amphibious craft, MTBs (otherwise known as PT boats), PCs, and SCs. Everywhere you look there are ships, some anchored singly and some nested together, and swarms of motor launches putter back and forth through the anchorage. It's just like Pearl Harbor, only five or ten times bigger. And the water is polluted, so you can get dysentery just by handling a line that's been over the side. We were directed to a watering station at a dock, which was fed by a stream coming out of the jungle, and over it was a sign: "This Water Polluted—Use At Your Own Risk." Doc Newman put bags of chlorine in the tanks while we were filling up, which make the water safe to drink but taste like hell. (The stream is polluted because Filipino families live along its banks farther up, and what they throw in the water could well be labelled Instant Death.)

The captain had to file a report about our action with the midget subs, and he spent a good deal of time today on the beach at Tacloban. He came back with the report that the cruiser *Indianapolis* is overdue, and was last reported in the same general area where we were attacked, so it's possible she ran into the same kind of trouble. (The theory is that the plane that tailed us, and the mother sub, were based on Formosa.) Nobody's sure, because there's been no definite word, but whatever happened doesn't sound good.

Another news item is that Churchill, Stalin, and President Truman (that name still sounds funny) met at Potsdam, Germany, and issued a statement calling for the unconditional surrender of the Japs. After what we've seen of their striking power, it doesn't seem likely they'll even bother to reply. All I can think of is what those midget subs could do to us during the invasion. I try not to think about it, but I sometimes wake up in the night seeing that boil of flame from the *Underhill*, and that leads me to what could happen to us. I think of that guy saying, "The whole world blew up," and I wonder that he had enough of his mind left to be able to talk. If I were in his place, I think I'd have been a jibbering idiot. Either that, or dead of fright.

Later—One final piece of hot news for the day: We got several bags of mail, and in it was a letter from Diane, saying she's married to Harry Coffin. It seems he was wounded at Iwo Jima, and when he was home on sick leave they got married. She wishes me all the luck in the world, and blah blah blah blah blah and all the rest of it.

I don't know what ever made me think I had a chance there in the first place, but it was nice to think about. It isn't easy to find new things to think about out here, and there's going to be a big blank in my daydreams until I can come up with something worthwhile. I saw a goat today, while we were taking on water, but there's no profit thinking about goats for very long. Maybe I should forget all that, and become an inventor. Maybe I should just hit the sack, and say the hell with everything.

Aug. 4—We're under a new command now; instead of being part of the Third Fleet we're AdComPhibsPac, which in plain English means Administrative Command, Amphibious Forces Pacific. They're the ones who actually get the troops ashore, and they're the ones who'll train us for our part in the operation. We train somewhere here in the Philippines, then start assembling—probably around Okinawa—for the jump onto Kyushu. You hear so much scuttlebutt it's hard to know what to believe, but one word is that we'll hit a couple of the smaller islands south of Kyushu first, and then go for the place itself. No matter what we do they'll still have those midget subs all around, not to mention the kamikaze planes, so what with one thing and another I don't see how any of our first wave can survive. I'll be one up on Harry Coffin as far as action goes, but a fat lot of good that'll do me. I wonder how Diane will react when she hears . . . oh, knock it off, Bowers. The invasion's three months away; don't kill yourself quite yet. What was that line Miss Gresham taught us? From somewhere in Shakespeare. . . . "Cowards die many times before their deaths; The valiant never taste of death but once." Try to remember that, whenever you start sniveling. Go ahead—try. Now try again.

Every now and then, a little ray of cheer shows up. The

operations manual for the invasion was brought aboard by armed messenger today, and it looks to be the size of the New York telephone book. I heard the captain and Mr. Gonnick discussing it in the wardroom, and Mr. Gonnick said he'd seen a copy of the Japs' plan for the defense of Guam. It was, he said, in three parts, each a sentence long. Part one said, "The enemy will precede his attack on Guam with a bombardment from the sea." Part two said, "During this bombardment, the forces of the Emperor will retire to cover," and part three wound it all up, "Following the bombardment, the forces of the Emperor will emerge from cover and victoriously drive the enemy into the sea." End of defense plan. Our plan, on the other hand, has fire-control grids for all the beaches; it outlines in every detail the steps for reaching those beaches; it had a section on what to do in case we have to retire; it has a section on the burial of the dead and the delivery of mail —in short, it spells out every possible emergency and how to cope with it, and if nothing else it's a comfort to know that somewhere in the rear areas people have given this a lot of thought. I'd hate to be killed in something that was sloppily conceived.

August 6—Another ray of cheer today. I was just coming out of the head when I ran into Caulkins, on his way down. "Did you hear?" he said. "They dropped an atomic bomb."

"Who did?" I replied. All I could think of was the rumor that the Germans had had one, and my first thought was they'd given it to the Japs.

"We did," said Caulkins. "It's like two thousand tons of TNT."

"Two thousand *tons*?" My mind tried to imagine it.

"Something like that."

Caulkins disappeared into the head, leaving me with my

thoughts. The way I see it, this may make the invasion a little easier. If we've got enough of these things, we can plaster the beaches before we go in, and if they're as powerful as they say then the defenses ought to be pretty well softened up. It might not get the people in the caves, but it would sure as hell give a jolt to the first line of defense. Whether it would do anything to the midget subs, remains to be seen.

Aug. 7—The dust still hasn't settled where we dropped that bomb, so it's hard to tell what it did. The place was called Hiroshima, for whatever that may be worth.

Aug. 9—We dropped another one today, this time on Nagasaki, so it looks as though we've started the softening-up process already. If we keep on at this rate until invasion time, we may have it easier than we thought.

Late flash: The Russians declared war on Japan yesterday, which should be another big help. Now, instead of concentrating everything on our invasion forces, the Japs are going to have to watch their right flank, or the Russians'll be at them by way of China and Korea. I'm glad I'm not the Emperor. (I remember, a year or so ago, writing that you could always find someone worse off than you, but I never thought it'd be the Emperor of Japan. I guess it just goes to show you never can tell.)

Aug. 10—Today was pretty much like any other, although the events of the last few days have made people a little more cheerful. (On the non-cheerful side, it turns out the *Indianapolis* was sunk, by midget subs, with some terrible loss of life—only about 300 survivors out of a crew of more than 2,000. The guys on the *Underhill* were lucky by comparison.)

We had the usual two-thirds liberty, with the liberty party going over to the recreation area on the beach, and then everyone came back to the ship for supper and a movie. (The movie was Fred Astaire in "The Sky's the Limit," which I'd seen at home with Diane and which I didn't feel like seeing again.) The captain had met an old friend on the beach and gone off to the battleship *Texas* for supper, so Mr. Murray was senior officer aboard. I was sitting in the radio shack with Altschuhl, when suddenly the radio opened up and an excited voice said, "All ships—all ships— now hear this: The Japanese have decided to accept the terms of the Potsdam Conference! I repeat—" He was cut off as Altschuhl switched to the p.a. system and relayed the message throughout the ship, and I ran outside and found everyone standing up and jumping and cheering. Then I looked around, and the whole of Leyte Gulf, as far as I could see on all sides, was blazing with a bright, steady light; every ship in the anchorage was shooting off its rockets, flares, and signal lights, and splashing the air with searchlight beams. The separate flares rose and fell and went out, but there were so many thousands of them that they gave off a solid glow, like the glare of lights over a city.

Van Gelder, the leading petty officer, made his way through the shouting men to Mr. Murray, and said, "Sir— request permission to break out the liberty beer." We carry a couple of dozen cases of beer, for use in places where there's none to be had on the beach, and since there's no drinking aboard ship it's kept under lock and key at all times. Mr. Murray paused for just a second, then gave his permission. It took a while to find the keys, but Mr. Murray finally located them, and Van Gelder took an eager work party below.

I went back into the radio shack, where the voice radio was a shambles of several different operators trying to speak at once. The senior admiral in the area was trying to stop the fireworks, and his radioman was having hard going getting the message across. In fact, he could barely complete a sentence, and what I heard was:

"Ah have a message for all ships; this is an all-ships message—"

"Take your all-ships message, and blow it through your hat."

"Get that accent. Where yo'-all from, Sparkie?"

"He fum Geo'gia. Cain't yo' tell?"

"Ah have a message—"

"Leave us alone, can't you, boy? We're all going home pretty soon now."

"That's what you think. I still got two years left."

"Why, you sad bastard. That'll teach you to be USN."

"Attention, all ships. Ah have an all-ships—"

"Hey, All-Ships, are you USN, too?"

"Hell, no. Ah have a—"

"Then shut up. You're going home like the rest of us."

"Listen, fo' Chras sakes, the admiral says knock off the pyrotechnics."

"The *what?*"

"Hey, All-Ships, how do you spell 'pyrotechnics'?"

"Peter-Yoke-Roger-Oboe-Tare—Honest, fellows, ah'm not kidding. The admiral says—"

"Write us a letter about it. We'll get it in the morning."

The liberty beer was all gone by the time the captain arrived. He came in a motor launch from the *Texas*, which had dodged the falling flares across the three or more miles that separated the battleship from us. Mr. Murray met him at the rail and told him about the beer, while the rest of us waited to see what his reaction would be. He went below, and reappeared with a bottle of bourbon, which he handed to Van Gelder.

"Put this where it'll do the most good," he said, and they shook hands and the captain went into the wardroom.

The door between the radio shack and the wardroom was open, and Altschuhl and Caulkins and I could see that all the officers were in there, plus Green and Lincoln, the Steward's Mates. It was a tight fit, because the wardroom and pantry together are about the size of the men's room in an Esso station, but they managed it, and they managed to put down two bottles of champagne Mr. Potter had been saving for Christmas. The captain gave Green the last of his champagne, and Green knocked it back in one swallow, then turned to Lincoln and said, "Lincoln, get off your ass and get some more liquor for the officers."

Lincoln drifted out into the night, and Mr. Donath went to the pantry refrigerator and brought out what looked like a bottle of maraschino cherries. He passed them around, and when anyone refused a cherry he suggested they try the juice, which, it turned out, was brandy. It lasted almost no time at all. Then Mr. Donath launched off into a story about a summer job he'd had pumping gas somewhere in Virginia, and how he'd been held up one night by three guys in a car with Kentucky plates. The story rambled a bit, and he was interrupted when someone got to our five-mile bullhorn, on the flying bridge.

"Step right up, you lucky lucky people," the bullhorn roared. "You are just in time to buy a brand-new second-hand PC boat. . . . What's that, lady? Three dollars and fifty cents? Lady, the paint alone is worth more than that. Do I hear four? Will someone bid me four dollars?" I recognized Linkovitch's voice.

"Maybe we'd better tone that down," the captain said, and started for the door. He was met by Van Gelder, who said, "Captain, we've made a little punch out here. We thought maybe you'd like to try some." The captain hesitated, then several of the guys gathered around and hoisted him on their shoulders, and we all trooped back to the 40-millimeter gun tub, where the rest of the crew were gathered around a large washbasin. It had begun to rain, and everyone was wet, but nobody seemed to take much notice. They put the captain down by the basin, then stood around, grinning, while someone handed him a ladle. He dipped it into the "punch," raised it in salute, then took a sip. His first reaction was as though someone had hit him in the mouth, but he tried not to show expression as he finished the drink and handed the ladle back. I noticed, however, that he let a lot of the liquid run down his chin, hoping that the rain would cover it up. He then thanked everyone and returned to the wardroom, having forgotten what he'd originally come out to do. Linkovitch had tired of the bullhorn, anyway, and was down with the rest of us waiting his turn at the ladle.

When it came my turn to drink, I saw why the captain had reacted as he did. The "punch" was equal parts grapefruit juice and 198-proof alcohol, which Napier had contributed from the gyrocompass stores. It burned my mouth like a blowtorch, and I was able to swallow only the smallest sip. Others, however, gulped it down like Coke. The rain stopped, or at least I think it did, and the evening developed into a general community sing. Robbins got to work on his guitar, while some guys sang in groups and some sang alone; some took various officers aside and told them that, as officers, they weren't too bad; and one or two tried to Indian wrestle with Mr. Chilton.

He beat them easily, then went up to the signal bridge and tried to set off a flare, but couldn't make it work.

Along about midnight the flares, which had continued steadily since the first announcement, began to die down, and the celebration became quieter. The captain and Mr. Murray and Van Gelder got the more paralyzed members of the crew below and into their bunks, and then checked around the ship to make sure things were more or less in order. I saw the captain go up to Robbins, who was standing at the rail and looking forlornly out at the flickering lights, and I could hear the captain ask him what the trouble was.

"I don't want to go home," Robbins replied, clutching his guitar in both hands.

"Why not?" the captain asked.

"You wouldn't understand, Captain." Robbins began to pick at the rail with one hand. "You never been a bum."

"That's a matter of opinion," the captain said. "It depends on whom you talk to."

"I don't mean that," Robbins said. "I mean a real bum. I was a bum before I joined the Navy, and I did things I don't even want to think about. I robbed, and I—" He was aware that Mr. Donath had joined them, and he switched the sentence and went on, "I got a crippled sister —she was crippled in a railroad accident—and I got to take care of her. Like that, I can't make enough money for myself to be anything but a bum. Or a—whatever." He didn't look at Mr. Donath, and Mr. Donath didn't say anything.

The captain tried a few encouraging words but Robbins wouldn't listen, and after a while the captain moved off. Mr. Donath lingered a couple of seconds more, then he, too, went away. I wondered how I could be of some comfort but there was nothing I could think of, so I went in search of Caulkins who, the last I'd seen him, was trying to compose a poem including the names of all the Presidents. I didn't find him, but at the rail just outside the wardroom door the captain was talking to Lincoln, who seemed to be crying. His head was bowed, and he gripped the rail with both hands.

"I don't understand what you mean," the captain was saying.

"Green pulled rank on me," Lincoln replied, in a clogged voice. "That's what I mean. He pulled rank."

"How did he do that?"

"He told me to get off my ass and get some more liquor for the officers," Lincoln said. Green appeared out of the wardroom, and Lincoln turned to him. "There you are, you bastard," he said. "You pulled rank on me."

"I didn't pull no rank on you," Green said. "What you talking about?" His voice was low, and ominously soft.

"You told me get off my ass and get some more liquor for the officers," Lincoln said.

"Sure I tell you get off your ass and get some more liquor for the officers," Green said. "That ain't pulling no rank on you."

"You pulled rank on me, you bastard," said Lincoln. "That's just what you did."

Green moved closer to him.

"Wait a minute," the captain said. "Lincoln, you shouldn't resent being told to do something—everyone in the Navy has to take orders from someone, and if you worry about it you'll drive yourself crazy. You have to take it from Green, he has to take it from me, I have to take it from the unit commander, and so on up the line. We're all going home pretty soon anyway, so if you can put up with it just a little longer everything'll be all right. Just don't let it get you down. O.K.?"

Lincoln made a loud sniffling noise.

"Will you try to remember that?" the captain said. "Try to remember it's nothing personal—it's just the system."

"I'll try," Lincoln said.

"Good." The captain went below and Green drifted off, but Lincoln stayed at the rail, crying like a small child.

Aug. 11—Well, it seems the war isn't over, after all. The Japs want to make sure they keep their Emperor, and the Allies say there can be no conditions. So where are we? Back where we were yesterday morning.

Aug. 12—There's some kind of negotiating going on, but it doesn't seem to be getting anywhere. We get the news over the Fleet radio, and it comes in at dictate speed, so what we hear is: "The Imperial Government of Japan . . . the Imperial Government of Japan . . . meeting in extraordinary session yesterday . . . meeting in extraordinary session yesterday . . . announced there would be no change in their demand . . ." and so on. It's enough to drive you crazy, especially when they don't say anything. If anyone wants to keep this war going, they're more than welcome to come out here and take over.

Aug. 13—More of the same. For a minute there I thought we weren't going to have to make the invasion, but I guess that was just spitting into the wind. If I stay in the Navy long enough, I may learn better than to count on anything.

Aug. 14—Today we moved from Tacloban up to Samar, which is the island just north of Leyte. In the early afternoon it came over the radio that the Emperor has finally surrendered, and will stay on as head of the Japanese

Government, under our control. Only one person had any reaction other than a long sigh, and that was Mr. Chilton. He said, "Hot damn—now for the Russians!" and he had the bad luck to say it in the captain's hearing. The captain whirled on him, and I have never in my life heard an officer take such a chewing out. The captain chewed his ass all the way up to the third rib and back down the other side, and when he was through Mr. Chilton was red in the face and kind of dazed. (The captain, on the other hand, had turned white.) There was a short silence, and then Mr. Chilton said, "Will that be all, sir?"

"For now," the captain replied, and Mr. Chilton vanished. The captain looked at the rest of us, and said, "I'm sorry. That should have been done in private."

"Think nothing of it, sir," said Caulkins. "We enjoyed it."

Sept. 2—Today is the day the Japs officially surrender, on board the *Missouri* in Tokyo Bay. We've been fruiting around in the Philippines while AdComPhibsPac tries to think of what to do with us, and the latest word is that we're going to escort a group of LSTs full of Occupation troops up to Japan, by way of Okinawa. I suppose there could be worse duty, and now we've come this far we might as well see the place that all the shooting was about. (Since nobody knows what the reactions of the frustrated kamikazes will be to our appearing in their home waters, there's been some question as to what kind of precautions we should take. The word now is that we should hold our fire unless they attack first, when we should then "shoot them down in a friendly fashion.")

Treadway, our draftee, is already asking for a hardship discharge, claiming his wife is pregnant. He should talk to Napier, who hasn't heard from *his* wife since that letter announcing her condition.

Sept. 20—So here we are, escorting a dozen LSTs up to merry Okinawa and typhoon country. One thing the typhoons have done, and we hear this on the Fleet radio, is stir up the minefields, and the waters around Japan are a mess of floating mines. Our sweepers have been clearing lanes through the fields, but then a typhoon comes along and louses everything up, and there's no telling where the mines may be. It could get kind of hairy, if something isn't done.

Oct. 3—We were in Okinawa long enough to have to sortie for another typhoon, and now we're on our way to Japan. The waves in the wake of the typhoon are like mountains, and at night it's practically impossible to see anything that might be floating in the water. We can now keep our running lights on, however, and they make a slight glow around us, but I'm not sure this is a good thing. Last night Bessinger saw what he swears was a mine sliding right past the side of the ship, but by the time he could report it it was gone, and the captain wasn't about to go back and look for it in the darkness. If Bessinger hadn't seen it we'd have been none the wiser; now everyone is sweating. But you can sweat for just so long, and then you have to think of something else.

Oct. 5—We got our first look at Japan today, through a cold, drizzling rain, and all we saw was a bleak mountain rising out of the sea. Everything else was mist and rain, and Humma, who'd been checking the recoil cylinder on the 3-inch gun, stared at the scene for a while in silence.

"My God," he said, at last. "No wonder so many Japanese come to America."

We headed in Bungo Suido, which is the entrance to the Inland Sea, and here we ran into another problem: there were the usual floating mines, but there were also several fields of pressure mines, which our birdmen had dropped. These were detonated by the water pressure of a ship passing over them, and in dropping them we broke one of the first rules of mine warfare, which is you don't sow a mine you don't know how to sweep. We had no idea how to sweep these things; we'd set them to go sterile in late November, when we figured our invasion forces would be clear of the area, and in addition to that the birdmen weren't very clear as to exactly where they'd dropped them. They'd been in something of a hurry, and besides there are no decent charts of the area, so the only clue they could give was they'd dropped them "somewhere along there," or "sort of near that thing with twin peaks." So what we had to do was go very slowly, as though on tiptoe, around the areas where the mines might be, and hope for the best. We sank three floating mines with rifle fire, and nobody set off a pressure mine, so all in all we were lucky.

The first thing that struck me, when I could get a good look at Japan, was how much it looks like Japanese prints. I'd always thought they were kidding, with those queer-looking trees, and mountains coming out of the water and everything, but by God they mean it. It's just what they look like.

Oct. 7—Our anchorage is at Hiro Wan, an area about twenty miles south of Hiroshima and near the naval base at Kure. There's a big Japanese battleship resting on the bottom, sunk by our carrier planes, but all the other ships are American, and it's the usual assortment. I don't know how many hundreds or thousands of ships we have in the

Pacific, but I think if the Japs could have seen that Fleet Organization Book they might have surrendered sooner than they did. Their navy took up barely one page in our Naval Intelligence bulletin; ours, as I've said, needed a book the size of a phone directory.

Oct. 9—Typhoon Louise has hit Okinawa, and seems to be headed this way. Being in an inland sea we can't sortie as we usually do, so the captain ran the ship into a cove protected on three sides by high hills, and put out two anchors to keep us from dragging. All day and all night we heard distress calls on the radio, from ships at Okinawa that were being driven up on the beach or capsized or whatever, and from the sound of it the damage was terrible. Whole Quonset huts took off in the air, and ships were breaking up right and left. Then the wind began to pick up here, but the mountains around us were high enough to break the force of the storm, and we had no damage. But Kyushu, the southern island we'd been going to invade, took a heavy pasting. I hate to think what would have happened if we'd been gathering for the invasion when that thing struck.

Oct. 10—This morning was bright and clear, and our ship had swung around to within a couple of hundred yards of the beach. We saw a lone Japanese, standing by his bicycle and staring at us, and we could almost read his thoughts. Here, in front of him, was a ship from the conquering Navy; it was a seedy little bucket covered with rust and zinc chromate, with laundry hanging from the lifelines and the boat boom, the crew mostly in underdrawers and shower clogs, scratching themselves while they drank coffee and smoked cigarettes and coughed and spat and peed over the side. We were about as military looking as a convention of cod fishermen, and to this Japanese it must have been the depth of humiliation. He looked at us for several minutes, then remounted his bike and rode slowly along the path and out of sight.

Oct. 12—They've set up a point system for return to the States. The captain is eligible, but he has to wait for a replacement with orders to relieve him, and while Mr. Murray will probably get command it'll still be a little while. Several of our enlisted men, including Pin-Head, are eligible, and a message came over from the Operations Officer saying there's a ship leaving tomorrow that'll take them back as far as Guam. I think what I may do, just to be on the safe side, is give these pages to Pin-Head to give to Miss Gresham, and that way I'll be sure of her getting them. Nobody knows how long I may have to wait, and I'd just as soon she got them as soon as possible. She'll probably want to fool around with the wording, because there've been times when I've been more intent on getting something written than I have in making it sound pretty. Then, of course, there are probably times when I was so intent on sounding pretty that I forgot to say what happened.

At any rate, she'll know what to do.

* * *

July 1, 1946—I've only just now finished going over Ralph's diaries, partly because of the pressure of school work and partly because at first I didn't want to look at them. I was afraid of them, but now, having read them all, I see my fears were groundless. I haven't changed a word (I must admit the temptation was strong to soften some of his remarks about me), and although I offered to let his family see them, they were too overcome to want any further reminders of their son. Perhaps in the course of time, if these are ever published, they will be able to read them with the proper detachment and a feeling of pride. According to the newspaper there was one survivor of the explosion, a boy by the name of Lincoln who was, for some reason, up in the mast at the time, and it's possible he might be able to offer a few extra details. But I'm sure there are many people wanting to talk to him, and I would be the last to impose on his time. In the final analysis this is Ralph's story, and he is the one who should be telling it.

Millicent R. Gresham